TABLE OF CONTENTS

DEDICATION

This book is dedicated to all of the people that make me want to be a writer.

Rod Serling, he was the first that not only made me want to write, he taught me about imagination

But many others followed……In no particular order

Lester Bangs, Dave Marsh, John Steinbeck, Ernest Hemingway, Stephen King, Cormac McCarthy, Hunter Thompson, Greg Pearson, Enoch Needham, Todd Schack, Chris Hartman, Damon La Scala, Jim Carroll, Mike Ness, Rod Stewart, Bob Seger, Alice Cooper, Iggy Pop, My Chemical Romance, Pink Floyd, Ray Davies, Joan Jett, Axl Rose, Herman Hesse, Brett Easton Ellis, Fyodor Dostoevsky, P.J. O'Rourke, Allan Weisbecker, Dan Ackroyd, Quentin Tarantino, Edgar Allan Poe, Richard Bach, George Orwell, Aldus Huxley, Joyce Carol Oates, Ken Kesey, Tom Robbins, Douglas Coupland, Elmore Leonard, Don Henley, Steve Earle, Willie Nelson, Paul Simon, Johnny Cash, Tom Petty, Stevie Nicks, Billy Joel, Neil Diamond,

Randy Newman, Lou Reed, Brian Wilson, Neil Young, Leonard Cohen,

Jimmy Breslin, Franz Kafka, Charles Bukowski, And... Dr. Seuss

I

Destination

Dimitrios looked in the rearview mirror. There was a fragment of

somebody's bone above his eyelid, plastered there in dried blood. There

were other specks of dried blood on his face that made his face look

freckled. The speedometer was a steady 110 miles per hour. He looked

at the world outside the windows and realized that he had no idea where

he was. Steep, jagged mountains rose up all around him, some of which

had snow on their peaks. The air coming through the truck vents, was

cool, but stagnant.

There was something coming towards him. As he got closer, he

could see that it was a group of bikers. He looked in the rearview mirror,

and saw that there was another group of bikers following him. All of the

riders were dressed the same. They wore black leather jackets and had

blue scarves wrapped they're around their heads. Each of them, had their faces covered in red bandanas. They looked more like an army than they did a gang.

When he was coming up on the bikers, they left him nowhere to go except a two-lane blacktop heading northwest. He turned down the road to see if the bikers would follow him. To his relief, the two groups stopped, and watched as his car drove towards the mountains. The relief subsided and a sense of fear overcame him but he didn't know what he supposed to be afraid of.

He drove slowly, keeping his eyes on the bikers. There was a caravan of pick-up trucks driving up from the south with flags waving in their beds. They were being led by a police vehicle, it's lights were flashing, but Dimitrios couldn't hear any sirens. The bikers dismounted and pulled guns from the back of their bikes. They did it in unison making it look like some type of military operation. The caravan of trucks slowed, and eventually stopped.

Dimitrios wasn't even aware that the car radio was on until the music was interrupted by a top of the hour news update. The announcer came through the speakers saying that a nationwide search was underway for a suspect accused of shooting eight people at a casino in Las

Vegas, Nevada. Authorities did not know the name of the suspect, or have any clue about him, only that he was believed to be driving an older model Dodge Ram pickup truck. It was last spotted on Highway 491 near Cortez, Colorado. He turned off the radio.

It became apparent to him that the bikers were escorting him somewhere. Something caught his eye off to the side of the road. It was a man sitting on a horse. Dimitrios slowed the truck down to get a better look. It was an old Indian chief sitting on a silver horse with black spots. The man had on a headdress with feathers that formed a crown above his weathered face. He wore a suit made of leather that was decorated with more feathers. It struck Dimitrios that there was no color to the figure. He looked like an old black and white photo. The chief had no expression on his face as Dimitrios drove by.

More bikers showed up, seemingly out of nowhere. They were on a road that curved for no reason, and were driving towards a grove of trees. They were behind Dimitrios, and ahead of him. A hand carved wooden sign greeted him as he entered the town of Crestone, Colorado. As he drove through, he couldn't help but notice the unique architecture. There were round homes, and some of the buildings looked like they were space ships. The term "spiritual center" was on signs outside many of the structures. One building in particular made him stop and look. It was an old cabin, at least a century in age, it had once been painted white, but only yellowing streaks of the color were left, the rest of it was weathered wood. A giant inflatable spider had been in attached to the corner, making it look like the creature was crawling out of a time warp.

On the far edge of town, Dimitrios drove in front of a building that he figured was some type of temple. It looked like something that you would see in the Far East like Thailand or Nepal. It was a hot springs resort of some type. As he was sitting in the car looking at the place, a woman walked out of the front door. She had a Mona Lisa smile on her face. Her hair was curly and wild. What looked like a blouse, was actually a full sleeve tattoo on her arm. He was too far away to see what the design was.

The woman made direct eye contact with the Dimitrios. She shook her head as if to say "no". She pointed her finger to a dirt road in the distance that headed up into the mountains. He looked toward the road, and then looked back towards the woman. She had her back turned to him and was walking back inside the building.

With a strong sense of hesitation, Dimitrios followed the dirt road for a few miles until it came to a dead end. A lone biker sat there watching him. The biker pulled some brush away, revealing what was probably a old stage coach road at some time. In the distance, up on the side of the hill was a house. The morning sun was rising above the mountains behind it.

"I guess this is where I'm supposed to be going," he said to himself. "My destination".

II

The Rising Dust

Before Sam Coyote even saw the truck, he could see the plume of dust rising through the trees and coming in his direction. He heard the sound of the truck stopping and shifting into four-wheel drive. He stood in the parlor window of his house on the hill and watched until the truck came into view. He bowed his head for a moment. He knew this day would come at some point.

The road up to Sam's house had several little areas to the pull off. They were littered with old RVs. Each one had a ritualistic fire pit, and motorcycles out front.

Every night for two weeks Sam had awoken at

exactly 3:16 am. He felt compelled to go for walks. The first

night it happened he was walking through the sagebrush,

when a perfect circle of fire formed around him. He watched

the flames, and had a vision of himself in the sky, flying, like

he was a bird. "This isn't the real fire," the vision said. "The

real inferno comes shortly". With that the flames died out. A

bear bawled in the trees not too far away.

Most of the times Sam Coyote went on those walks,

there were orbs of light that would hover above his head.

The colors of the lights were ever changing. They would

move back and forth in a southwest direction. Sam Coyote

had been in the San Luis Valley for many years and had seen

lights in the sky countless times, but the orbs on his walks

seemed to be following him, as if they were monitoring his

every step. Sam Coyote felt like the orbs were inviting him

somewhere, but he was reluctant to accept the invitation.

He sensed that change was imminent, he could feel it in his bones. The valley that he had known his entire life was in subtle disarray. The place had always been a little odd, but he had never experienced anything there that he thought might harm him. In those early morning hours, he wasn't so sure about that anymore. There was an energy shift taking place.

The truck came to a stop outside the window where Sam Coyote was watching. A robust man who was maybe in his late thirties or early forties got out of the truck. He was wearing a white uniform that had numerous dark stains on it. The arriving stranger had closely cropped brown hair and a goatee. He was built sturdy, and might have been an intimidating sight if he didn't look so bewildered. After he closed the door to the truck, the man stood there and stared up at the window where Sam Coyote was watching.

After a few moments, the stranger started walking up the hill toward the dwelling. Sam Coyote looked at the baseball bat in the corner, but as he watched the man nothing struck him as threatening. If anything, Sam Coyote thought, the guy looked as if he were lost. There was a look of confident curiosity on his face. He kept playing with his phone.

Sam Coyote wasn't sure if he had even been noticed yet. He walked through the doorway and stood on the porch. The stranger took a few moments before he noticed Sam. When he did, he stopped in his tracks. They stared at each without saying a word, unsure what to make of one another.

"There is no cell phone coverage in this valley. The companies say they don't know why, which usually means the military is nearby. Can I help?" Sam Coyote finally said.

"My name is Dimitrios".

"Sam Coyote". Dimitrios sized him up, he was maybe six foot, with a muscular physique, long flowing brown hair with a neatly trimmed beard. His white linen shirt enhanced his olive skin,

Dimitrios didn't say anything. He turned around and looked out over the valley below him, and then up at the Sangre De Christo Mountains towering behind the house. "Is there something I can do for you?" Sam asked again.

"I don't know," Dimitrios answered. "I'm not sure where I am. I'm not even sure how I got here".

"Are you lost?"

"No." Dimitrios stared at Sam Coyote. "I think I'm supposed to be here. There was a lady in town that pointed me this direction. I'm not sure why"

As Sam Coyote looked at Dimitrios, he wondered if dark stains on his uniform was blood. It looked like it was on Dimitrios' face and hands as well. He wasn't sure who the woman was that pointed Dimitrios in his direction, but he had a good idea.

"Are you hurt?" Sam Coyote asked.

"I'm okay. Do you know who I am?"

"I have an idea of who you might be, but I can't say for certain."

"The last thing I remember was being is being in Las Vegas, but now that I'm here I feel like I'm somebody else".

Sam Coyote knew exactly what that feeling was like. It was something he had felt his entire life.

III

The Drive In

"Get back in the truck", Sam Coyote told Dimitrios. "I think you are almost in the right place, but not quite".

"What do you mean?"

"I'll get you there".

Dimitrios walked back down to the truck and got behind the steering wheel. Sam wasn't sure of his wisdom, but he opened the passenger door and got in. "Go back the way you came in," Sam Coyote said. The two rode in silence until the truck reached a dead end in the town of Moffat at Highway 17. A lone biker was following them. Dimitrios asked Sam who the bikers were. "Make a left," was the response he got.

Dimitrios did as his passenger told him. "Where am I?" Dimitrios finally asked Sam.

"Where do you think you are?"

"I don't know. Something strange happened. I was on Interstate 40, not sure exactly where I was going, I knew that I needed to be driving. Driving fast. I needed to be as far away from Las Vegas as I could get. I remember seeing a sign that said 'Welcome to New Mexico. The land of enchantment'. Right after that, the wind came up. It kicked up a lot of dust. A big group of bikers appeared out of the dust. I couldn't see anything except for them. I was about to pull over, when a strong gust hit me sideways. It shook the truck so hard that I thought I was going to roll it. I realized that I couldn't stop, the truck was driving itself. A man that I recognized, his name was Byron, was sitting in a truck on the side of the road watching me. I wasn't sure, but the bikers signaled north up the road. Then, like I crossed through some barrier, then wind and dust were gone. It was suddenly a beautiful calm day. I wasn't on the interstate anymore. After a few miles, I saw a sign that said Highway 491."

"491?" Sam Coyote asked.

"That's what the sign said. I passed through a town called Shiprock...."

"Oh," Sam remembered. "You were on the old Highway 666. The Devil's Highway they used to call it. I forgot that they renumbered it a few years back. People these days want to whitewash history if there is something that offends them."

"I think they want us to be lost."

Sam Coyote looked at the driver, puzzled by his words. He ignored the comment and looked back at the road. "Well, when you travel the Cosmic Highway anything can happen. When you come to the town of Hooper make a right".

"Okay." Dimitrios looked around and saw what appeared to be a white dome with scaffolding around it. What's that?"

"The UFO watchtower. There's a lot of people that come to this valley to go there. An old lady named Margaret runs it. The sweetest lady you would ever want to meet. She knows everything there is to know about this valley."

Dimitrios kept driving where Sam told him to until they came to an old drive-in theatre a mile or two north of Monte Vista. Sam Coyote told him to pull into the parking lot of a motel that had balconies facing the drive-in screen. There was a permanent "No Vacancy" sign. "This was where you were supposed to drive too," Sam said.

Dimitrios looked at the two-story building that looked like it could collapse at any moment. Most of the paint had chipped away from the elements, and the curtains in all of the windows were well weathered. "This place looks abandoned," he said. "Is there anybody here?"

"They built a bigger and better one down on the big highway, but this one only looks abandoned," Sam Coyote told him. "And it only looks that way to you personally, think of it as optical illusion if that helps. There is so much more going on in that old place than you could ever know. Besides, I think the best place for you to be is where the outside world would think that its abandoned."

The two of them got out of the truck. "What am I supposed to do here?"

Sam pointed to a door that had some red spray paint on it. "You walk through that door. Once you're inside you should be able to figure everything else out. You'll have some questions, but in time things will start to make a little more sense".

Dimitrios looked into Sam's face unsure whether he could trust him or not. Could he trust himself? He looked over at the door, then back at Sam's face. Dimitrios smiled, "I guess I don't have much of a choice. I'm kind of hungry though."

Sam Coyote grabbed the keys to the truck out of Dimitrios' hand and said, "Don't worry about it. Once you walk through that door, you'll find that the rooms are well stocked. I'll take the truck back to my place and hide it." Sam handed Dimitrios a metal key. "That's to the room. I'll be back later." With that, Sam got into the truck and drove away.

When Dimitrios got to the door he saw that the red spray paint wasn't graffiti. It was an intricate painting of a fierce looking bird. He studied it for a few minutes and then walked inside.

"Talakugang" he said to himself. He didn't even know what that meant, but the word came to him.

IV

UFO Café

Lola was wondering where Sam was. When he drove up, he motioned her to come out with his finger. Lola was a beautiful girl in her early twenties, with long straight dark brown hair and eyes of the same color. There was a melancholy between them, Lola would soon be marrying Victor. Sam knew his days of being the only man in her life were waning.

"Let's go get something to eat", he said opening the passenger door for Lola.

"Who was that you left with Sam?"

"His name is Dimitrios. How did you know?"

"Sorry Sam, but there are no secrets. Something doesn't feel right," Lola said. "His name may be Dimitrios, but who is he?"

"I don't know who he is, but I think I've been expecting him for quite some time"

Lola gave Sam a harsh stare.

"What's that look for?" he asked.

Lola smirked and shook her head. "Sam, I heard he was covered in blood. Didn't you think that to be strange?"

"Yeah. The bikers brought him here though."

"And you welcome him here? What are the others going to say? You know that there is nothing good that can come from this."

"Look honey, I know that you worry about me and I appreciate it. The truth is, if he's who I think he is, there's no way I could have kept him from coming. Somebody called him here though."

Sam and Lola walked into the UFO café, the corrugated steel interior wasn't much to look at, but the "food was out of this world". That was the slogan on the sign out front. "Margret," Sam Coyote yelled out in the empty eatery. "You got a couple of customers out here who are need of a good old-fashioned meal".

Margaret came out of the kitchen at a pace you wouldn't expect from a woman of her age. Her hair was white, and a pair of bifocals hung from a strap around her neck. "Why Sam Coyote, it's about time you come in. You need to come down off that mountain more often." She gave him a quick a hug, but reached for Lola and gave her a long hearty one. "Lola, I swear you get prettier and prettier every time I see you."

"Awwweeee, thank you Aunt Margaret. That's sweet of you to say."

"You two sit down. I've got a surprise for you. There's a new meatloaf recipe I've been wanting to try on someone. And I couldn't think of a better pair than my two favorite people in the entire valley."

"That sounds delicious," Sam said as Margaret hurried back into the kitchen.

Sam and Lola sat down at the counter and looked up at the TV in the corner. An actress-like reporter on the screen holding a microphone and saying that a manhunt was underway for the suspect who had shot eight people to death in a Las Vegas casino. Police were saying that there was only a vague description of the shooter, and they didn't know the identities of the dead. They have no idea who the suspect is.

"Another day, another mass shooting," Sam said casually.

"Interesting," Lola said sarcastically. "The same day some random stranger shows up at your door covered in blood, we hear about a shooting not that far away. Does that seem like a coincidence to you?"

Before Sam Coyote could answer, Margaret was placing two plates of meatloaf and mashed potatoes on the counter in front of them. "I've been watching the news all day about this," Margaret said as she looked up at the TV. "They don't have a clue who did it. After I close up here, I'm going to run down to the Valley Courier and see what's coming in over the wire. I need to write a story for the morning paper"

"They'll find him," Sam said. "They always do."

"They don't always find them if somebody is hiding them," Lola said.

Sam was clearly irritated by the snarky tone and looked at Lola and nodded toward Margaret. "This is some damn good meatloaf Margaret, what makes the recipe so special?" he said to change the subject of the conversation.

"Green chile," Margaret said. "They're harvested them in New Mexico".

𝔙

The Seventies

Dimitrios looked around the room. It looked like something from a porn movie made in the seventies. The long thick drapes were made of red velvet. The carpet was shag but it was hard to be sure of the color since the room was illuminated only by a black light and a faint neon sign reading, "Hotel California – East". He tried to think of the lyrics to the Eagles song, wondering if there was a significance.

Beyond the room with the king size bed was another room. There was a small kitchen with a two-burner stove and a refrigerator, and a bathroom with only a toilet and a shower stall. On the back wall was an enormous wooden door with a big brass lever as a knob. Dimitrios studied the door for a moment; it seemed so out of place. He was curious about what was behind it, but needed a shower first.

As the water ran down Dimitrios' body it turned a light pink going down the drain. He had to hold his face directly to the hot water for an extended period of time before a bone fragment unstuck from his forehead. Even after he had rinsed off the soap, he let steam fill the room and breathed deeply.

He toweled dry, and noticed a clothes rack in the corner. There were shirts, pants, unopened packages of underwear and socks. The room had been perfectly designed for him. He looked in the refrigerator; it was filled with food, water, and even some liquor. The little cabinet above the stove was also had food in it. He looked around the room and wondered who would do this for him. Somebody knew that he was coming, even if he didn't know that himself.

Once dressed, he looked out the window. There were no other cars in the parking lot, yet he didn't feel as though he was only person in the motel. He noticed that there was no office, nowhere to pay for the room, but it was obvious that at least the interior of the motel was being maintained by someone. In front of the drive in's screen was a broken playground that hadn't seen a kid in years. A projection house sat in the middle of the poles where the speakers used to hang. He heard motorcycles riding up and down the road.

After he went back in, he once again studied the big wooden door at the back of the room. It seemed medieval to him. It wasn't like anything else like it in the room, it wasn't something that had been constructed lately. It was ominous to look at. He walked up and put his hand on the lever, but couldn't bring himself to turn it. He could feel an energy behind it.

Dimitrios went over to the refrigerator and pulled out a beer. He sat at the foot of the bed and continuously stared at the door. He laughed out loud to himself. He couldn't believe the angst a simple door was causing him. He finished the beer and quickly walked over to the door and turned the handle not allowing himself to think about what he was doing.

It was a tunnel. The walls made out of oversized stone blocks. There were dim lights every twenty-five feet or so. It smelled damp. He could see mold on the mortar between the blocks. Leaving the door open behind him, he started walking down the tunnel then noticed that it wasn't just a single tunnel, but a labyrinth of many tunnels. There was what seemed to be a main tunnel, with smaller tunnels that all appeared to end with doors identical to the one the Dimitrios had come through.

Dimitrios decided to explore the main tunnel later. The cosmic journey that had landed him in this strange valley had left him exhausted. He found his way back to the motel room and lay down on the bed. As much as he wanted to fall asleep, his mind was filled with a tidal wave of thoughts. How did he get there? Who was expecting him? The answers never came before he could no longer hold his eyes open.

VI

Sheriff Jack

"That motherfucking prick," Sam said to himself as he saw the flashing lights in the rearview mirror. The road into Crestone is two narrow lanes, he had to drive about half a mile before he could find a place to pull over.

He watched as Jack the sheriff exited the patrol car. The sheriff pulled a pack of cigarettes from his shirt pocket and lit one, standing there, surveying Sam's truck. Physically, Jack was not the imposing figure that you would expect from the face of the law in the valley. Though tall, he was on the abnormally skinny side. His uniform hung off of him, but it was always neatly pressed.

Although it didn't come from his physicality, Jack was not without intimidation, a calm demeanor masking chaos on the inside. When he first ran for sheriff, in his early twenties, he was way behind in the polls to Sheriff Walton who had been in office for almost thirty years and was going to run for one last term before retiring. About three weeks before the election, Sheriff Walton was elk hunting in the Cachetopa area near Salida when a high-powered bullet went through his brain. They never figured out what happened, they labeled it a "hunting accident". Jack barely won the election over a dead man. In two subsequent elections, Jack ran unopposed. There had been talk that he had a group of men who made sure there was nobody to run against him,

In his time since taking office Sheriff Jack had been involved into two fatal shootings, both of which were ruled "justified". A couple of other people had been wounded by one of his deputies. It's a rather high rate for a county with a low population and an even lower crime rate. To hear the Latinos of the valley tell it, Jack or one of his deputies will pull them over for the slightest perceived infraction. It was well known in northern part of the state, in cities like Denver, that blacks should be wary of traveling into the valley. Jack roughed up a few white people too.

After several puffs off of the cigarette, he tossed it into the road and walked quickly over to Sam's driver side window. "Hello Jack," Sam Coyote said. "We don't usually have the pleasure of seeing you this far up north in the valley. You're usually harassing motorists down on Highway 160."

"I came up here specifically to see you".

"Oh yeah. Why is that?"

"You seem to always know what's going on around here."

"If you say so."

"Have noticed anything strange going on in the valley? Or strangers?

"It's the San Luis Valley. There's always something strange going on here. It's been that way for centuries."

"I guess that's true," the sheriff said with a phony chuckle. "Did you hear about what happened in Las Vegas"?

"You mean those people getting shot?"

"Yeah."

"I saw something about it on the TV while I was having dinner at the UFO café. What does that have to do with me?"

"It doesn't have anything to do with you. They don't seem to know anything about who did it. I've been reading everything that's been coming through down at the station. The FBI is still looking for him in Nevada."

"Well, Jack, if this doesn't have anything to do with me, and I don't see how it has anything to do with you, please tell me why you pulled me over to have this conversation?"

Jack became visibly angry. "Those people that were murdered in that casino were my friends. They were fine people. They were right thinking people. Patriots"

"Look Sheriff, I'm going to ask you one more time, why are you asking me about this?"

"There something strange about this case. Like I said, they don't have a clue who did this. With all of the cameras covering every square inch of Vegas, that can't come up with a single image of the perp. It's as if ghost did it. And when I think of ghosts, or spirits, or weird fucked up shit, you're the first person I think of."

"So, you do think that I had something to do with it?"

"No, but my gut tells me that you, somehow, someway you know something about what happened. I'll never know what happened to that woman, a so-called medium, what's her name, that went missing last year, but I'll bet you know exactly where she's at"

The picture of the piece of bone stuck to Dimitrios' face came to Sam's mind. "I wish I could help you Jack, but I'm not sure you're thinking this through logically."

The sheriff smiled. "You could be right. My wife might even be right. She thinks a Mexican did it. One of those illegals that waltz right into this country to murder and rape our fine citizens. She says this kind of stuff wouldn't happen if there was a wall. She may only be a woman, but sometimes her thinking is spot on."

VII

The Lights

There were sounds at the Drive-In Inn. Multiple sounds, a humming, high-pitched beeping sounds, and a swooshing noise that seemed to have some type of pattern to it, like Morse code. Dimitrios thought about the wisdom of checking what they were.

Flashing lights were behind the closed curtains. He closed his eyes. "It's the cops", he whispered to himself. He thought about running through the door in the back and into the tunnel. He opened his eyes to the lights coming through the curtains. Those aren't cop lights he realized.

He got up and used his forefinger to slightly open the seam of the curtains. A single pulsating white light was hovering right above the drive-in screen. As he opened the curtains wider, he saw that it wasn't a single light, but three lights. Besides the white one, there is a pink one and a green one. The latter two were not are not as bright as the white one. As he pulled the curtains all the way open to watch the lights, they started moving.

The pink one, with its beeping sound, moved to above the right-hand corner of the theater screen, the green hummed to above the left-hand corner. The white one, with a loud whoosh moved toward the window Dimitrios was watching from. It seemed to be staring at him. "What the fuck are they"? He said out loud.

As the white one moved closer to the window, it went dark and images started to appear on the drive-in screen. The projection light coming from a caretaker's house sitting back from the screen. The image was grainy and jumpy as though it had been shot with an old super eight-millimeter camera, but he recognized his wife. It was right after he met her years ago, when they were high school seniors. She was walking by a river, smiling and laughing. Then, in a higher definition, there is an image of her looking exactly as she looked when he last saw her, but she was on a couch crying. A tear ran down Dimitrios' eye. He hated seeing her like that. There were men in uniforms and suits standing around her.

The images disappeared, and the white light was back on. It was stalking Dimitrios, then in an instant it is gone. The pink light moved to the window, and as its light faded a new set of images appeared on the screen. It's was a hospital room, there were lots of people around, people that Dimitrios vaguely recognized. The camera zoomed into a swaddled newborn baby. He knew that was his daughter, another child came into the picture. It was his son. The image then morphed to his kids at their current age. They too, like their mom were crying. When the screen went dark, the pink light went back to where it was.

The green light also moved towards the window. The images projecting onto the screen were all still shots. They were bodies. They were soaked in blood, their skin blue in color. Each body was photographed from various angles to capture every wound they suffered.

When the green light was gone, Dimitrios went to refrigerator and grabbed a beer and back to the window.

"What have I done? My family is so far away"

VIII

Moments of Clarity

Sam knocked on the big wooden door at the end of the tunnel. There was no answer. He knocked again. "Donovan it's me, Sam. Are you in there?" With still no answer, Sam Coyote turned the lever and the door opened. The smell of hash, and sitar music, permeated the room. In an antique chair by a stone fireplace was Donovan. His eyes slowly opened as Sam approached.

"Sam Coyote, my brother, how have you been? You don't get down to Ojo Caliente too often. You should get off of the Plane and out of the valley more."

"Donovan, you crazy bastard, how come you never come out of this place?" Sam looked around the room. There were pill bottles everywhere, hundreds and hundreds of them. There were as many empty bottles of Jack Daniels. "I see your maid took the week off."

Donovan slowly and feebly got up from his rocking chair. There were good days, and bad ones. He was wearing an only a bathrobe. For the past few years, that is all that Sam Coyote had ever seen Donovan wear. They had grown up together on the west side of Pueblo. Donovan was a year older than Sam, but anymore he looked to be fifty years older. The curly brown hair of his youth had fallen out a long time ago. Also gone was the athletic body that all of the girls in high school had loved, covered up by probably an extra hundred pounds of fat. The only semblance of his youth that remained were his sharp grey eyes.

"I'm getting by," Donovan said as he embraced his old friend. "My demons haven't killed me yet. Neither has the cancer"

"Are you killing them?"

"That is why I got out of the valley, after all this time, we seem to have come to an understating. Live and let live. Peace can last forever. Oh, and fuck Lilith"

Sam Coyote laughed. "I think the demon might have come for me."

"I heard that there might be a new monster up there."

"Are you talking about the guy at the Drive In Inn?"

"Yeah."

"Monster' is an interesting choice of words. Said his name is Dimitrios. I don't know what to make of him."

"He's changed the energy here."

"I like to think he may be lost. Showed up at my door. Said he didn't remember how he got there. He might not know why he is here, but I think I do."

"The story I hear is that he was covered in blood."

"Who told you that? Are far as I know, I was the only that saw him."

"Come on Sam, you've been in the valley long enough to know that there are eyes and ears everywhere. They're in the rocks. They're in the sagebrush."

"Yeah, I guess. The sheriff pulled me over yesterday. He didn't mention to Dimitrios by name, but somehow he thinks whoever shot all of those people in Las Vegas is here."

"The doctors have me on all kinds of shit," Donovan said. "They give me pills for depression. They give me pills for anxiety. I take shit that's supposed to make me anti-psychotic. That's for my brain. I don't how many other things I take that are supposed to be keep my organs from shutting down".

"I can tell," Sam said as he again looked around room.

"Every now and then, the drugs work perfectly in unison and I have moments of clarity. I feel like myself. I have visions."

"Did you know he was coming?"

"I knew something was coming. We both have demons from our past looking for us. Let's face it, we were not good people."

"When I saw his truck driving up the road to my place, I wasn't surprised. It was like I was expecting it."

"Something is changing. I don't know exactly what, or when, or anything like that, but you can feel it in the air. One thing I can tell you, Sam, is that he is by no means lost. He is here for a very specific purpose."

"I think you're right. I feel it too."

"Have you talked to Lilith about him?"

"I try to avoid Lilith whenever possible. Why do you think she would know anything about him?"

"Like I said, when the pills all come together right, and my mind is clear, I have visions and when I knew something was coming, she was in the vision."

"I had dinner with Lola the…."

"How is Lola?"

"She's good."

"Such a beautiful girl. That's one thing you did right in your life!

"She is a good kid. She told me she had a bad feeling about Dimitrios too."

"Then you don't need to hear anything from me, or Lilith, if Lola is suspicious, you should take that as gospel. She is destined for something important."

IX

A Man's Job

Sam Coyote took off his robe and slowly stepped into the hot springs. It was a ritual he tried to do at least twice a week, more if he could. There was something about sitting in the warm water that freed his mind. He usually tried to do it late at night when nobody else was around. There were medicinal powers to the water.

The pool of naturally warm water was big, the size of an Olympic pool. Most of the water was in a big room, that had windows all around it. There were several little side pools, even a couple of private rooms where the tourists weren't allowed. The smell of Sulphur could be overpowering at times.

Lilith was in the far corner of the springs with two young guys who couldn't have been out of their late teens. Sam didn't recall seeing them before. He had seen Lilith there many times with numerous men but she owned the place so she could do what she wanted. These two seemed to be the boys d'jour. She was taking turns kissing both of them.

Sam had been in the water for a few minutes before Lilith noticed him. She smiled and gave a playful, but devious sneer. She stood up in the waist high water to show off her breasts with pierced nipples. The water made her tattoos seem more colorful in the dim glow of the fire place near the water's edge.

Lilith told the two guys to stand up. She directed one of the guys to sit on the edge of the spring and then started playing with his dick. Before she started sucking him, she told the other guy to get behind and start fucking her. She looked over at Sam to make sure he was watching. The guys were simply too young. They both came before they even got started. Lilith became enraged at her lack of satisfaction.

"Jesus fucking Christ", she screams. "That was fucking horrible. What are you a couple of virgins?"

"Yeah," they both say simultaneously.

She shook her head and laughed. "Get the fuck out of here".

"But..." One of the guys tried to say.

Lilith pointed to the door. She wasn't laughing anymore. "I said get the fuck out of here".

The two guys remained still in the water. Sam laughed. Lilith glared at him for a moment, and then looks back at the two guys. Her voice became slow and measured. "If the two of you don't get the fuck out here, right fucking now, I swear to fucking God I will rip your balls off with my bare hands."

The two youngsters were terrified as they scrambled out of the water. They grabbed their clothes and literally run for the exit behind where Sam was soaking. Lilith yelled to them, "You can come back when you get a little more experience and learn not to blow your wads in less than a minute. She held up her hand with long black nails."

Lilith put her body in the water and slid through the liquid like a snake over to Sam. "Sorry Sam, I thought you were going to get a better show than that."

"I was hopeful for a while, but you can't expect boys to do a man's job."

"Well then, let's let THE man do his job". She straddled Sam without so much as giving him a kiss. She immediately started thrusting herself down on him to relieve her of the frustration she had felt only moments earlier. Sam let Lilith ride him until she started shuddering and moaning and finally reached the point where she is totally spent.

"Feel better?" Sam asked.

"Much," still trying to catch her breath. "I heard that some guy showed up at your door that the other day".

"How did you hear that?"

"Why do you think there are secrets here? You know how the Plane is. Word gets around. Is he one of us?"

"I don't know. There's something about him. I haven't figured it out yet."

"Where is he now?"

"Over at the Drive-In Inn. There's people here that think you are somehow the reason he is here."

"Who said that?"

"No names."

"I have been expecting somebody. I had a vision, but it wasn't very clear."

"Jack pulled me over the other day. He thinks the guy had something to do with shootings in Las Vegas."

"Yeah, well we all know what a fucking dick Jack is. All those psychedelic drugs he does are making him even more paranoid than he already was. Fucking prick."

"I didn't tell him anything about Dimitrios."

"Is that his name? Dimitrios?"

"Yeah."

"That does sound familiar. I don't know why, but it does."

"You know more than you're saying."

Lilith ignored his words. "Why don't we go back to my bedroom so we can fuck some more?"

"I can't. I got be up early to go fishing with Eugene in the morning."

X

Gutting Fish

Eugene's 1962 Chevrolet pickup truck labored its way up the mountain. The sun was about to come over the horizon. "They finally paved this road," he said to Sam. "I don't know if that's a good thing or not. When I first started bringing you up here as a boy, this was little more than an old stage coach road. You wouldn't see another soul around. Now with the asphalt down, it won't be long before the place is overrun with tourists".

"The whole state is being overrun by tourists".

"I know. It's a goddamn shame."

"I had dinner at the UFO café a few nights back, Margaret told me that all of the camping spots at the Sand Dunes are reserved for the summer."

Eugene parked the truck at the gate to a trailhead. He and Sam grabbed their fishing gear out of the back, and started walking up the trail. They weren't more than two hundred yards up when Eugene said he needed to sit down for a break.

"Maybe if you lost a hundred, hundred and fifty pounds, this hike would be a little easier for you," Sam said.

"It's not my weight, you smart ass, it's my bum knee. Don't worry. The fish will still be there if I sit down for a while. Besides, to lose that much weight wouldn't be any fun. Why would I deprive myself of what I love to eat? You only get one shot on this Plane of existence. Might as well enjoy every bit of it".

By the time the sun had cleared the peaks, there were four fishing poles with their lines in the water, two for each man. "We should take a picture," Eugene said. "There's not another person around. Might be the last time you ever see that."

"You might be right."

"Speaking of other people, it feels like our little Plane went up in population."

"You must be talking about Dimitrios."

"Is he at the Drive-In Inn?

"Yeah."

"I'll have to get over there and introduce myself. Maybe take him out for a drink or something."

"That could be interesting. Nobody else on the Plane knows what to make of him. They think its kind of odd that he shows up here out of the blue. I'm not so sure that's what he did"

"When you've been here as long as I have, you realize that's how everybody gets here."

"I never thought about it like that before, but you're right Eugene."

"Everybody is a stranger at first. You don't remember because you got here when you were so young."

"The first thing I remember is walking across the sand dunes with you. There was that strange sound."

"The soundtrack of the sand," Eugene smiled. "There are times when I like to go out there in the middle of the night and listen to it. It sounds like an orchestra of all violins. If it's just right I can sing Sinatra tunes along with it."

"I don't recall you telling me what caused that."

"I don't know. It's like everything else in this valley, on this Plane, all the strange things going on, I don't know what causes it. I don't want to know. I just ramble along with it. Enjoy it."

"You got one." Sam pointed to Eugene's fishing pole, the tip bending until it was almost in the water.

"Oh damn, this is a monster," Eugene said while reeling. "Shit, there's one my other line. Can you grab it?"

"No, I got one too."

For the next two hours, there was little time for conversation. The fish were biting as fast as Sam and Eugene could throw their lines back in. They had a bucket filled with rainbow trout, with a few bright red specked brook trout thrown in. "I'd say we've caught our limit and then some, Eugene said. "What do you say we get out of here and go to that little bar in Manassa for some beers?"

"Sounds like a plan. There's nothing quite like a few beers at ten in the morning."

"Sarcasm this early? Why don't you get ahold of Dimitrios and tell him to meet us there?"

"Nah, I want to find out a little bit more about him before I let him get too close."

"Suit yourself Sam. I'll take him out drinking in a few days. I'd like to see what he's all about too."

After the fish were gutted and on ice in the Igloo cooler, Sam and Eugene started the hike up over the ridge and down the trail back down to the truck. Eugene, as on the way in, had to stop and rest a few times. "One of these days, a hike like this is going to be the death of me."

XI

Liberty Trail

"We should probably have signed the registry. Just in case," Carey said with the typical frown on her face. Keith and Dean looked at each other and rolled their eyes.

"It's a half mile back down the trail," Dean said with a disgusted tone.

"I would feel safer," Carey said. She tried to do the sad puppy dog look, but the result was utterly annoying.

"Are you going to do it?" Keith asked.

"Goddamn it, I'll do it," Dean said taking off his back pack. Keith and Carey watched as Dean headed down the trail. He was so short, that sometimes they could not see him through the grass, but they could occasionally see his spikey brown hair bobbing up and down.

"He won't be back for a while." Keith took off his shirt showing a body covered with tattoos. He ran his hand across his receding hair line. "We have time for a quick fuck," Keith moved close to Carey.

"Not now Keith." Carey was not unattractive, just kind of plain looking. She could have a great sense of humor when she wasn't riddled with anxiety over some inconsequential thing.

"Come on."

"No. It's too early."

"How about a blow job?"

"Keith, please stop."

"You know you love my dick."

"Do you ever stop thinking about sex?"

"Not really."

Carey looked down the trail. "There's Dean."

"Okay the registry is signed," Dean said, still irritated as he put his backpack back on.

"That was quick," Carey said.

"I ran."

The three hikers made their way down Liberty Trail. They weren't expecting to come to a fork in the trail. Dean pulled out his map and told the other two that there isn't supposed to be a fork. They tried to take the trail on the left, but decided it didn't look beaten enough. They retraced their steps and took the right fork. Dean's compass pointed south which was the right direction. About an hour and a half later, they get to Deadman's Creek and stopped to rest to have some water.

"Mama!" A voice cried out. It sounded like a child.

"Geez, somebody brought a kid out here?" Keith says to the other two. The three of them stood up and to look around.

"Mama!" The voice cried out again.

"That sounds like a little kid, really little," Carey said.

"Let's go see what's going on," Dean said. They put their backpacks on and walked rapidly up the trail.

"Mama!"

"Fuck," Keith said. "How come nobody's answering?"

"Maybe there's been an accident, somebody's hurt."

They walked feverishly, yet alert, to find the voice. "Shit, something just ran across the trail up there," Keith said.

When they got to the spot where Keith saw whatever it was, they stopped and poked through the brush looking for the kid. "It was probably just a marmot," Dean said.

"That wouldn't be good for a kid," Keith says.

Carey, was up ahead on the trail, yelled back. "There's an old cabin up here."

"Maybe the kid is in there," Keith said.

"The voice didn't sound like it was coming from this direction," Dean said.

"We can't go anywhere without at least checking," Carey said.

"We should probably go back and tell somebody what we heard," Dean said.

"I'm going to go look," Keith said. "Come with me Dean."

As the two men were looking around the cabin for any sign of the child, they heard Carey scream hysterically. "Get out here now".

As the ran for the door, Carey was enveloped by a gigantic shadow. She stopped screaming, but a look of terror distorted her face. Dean and Keith looked up in the sky to see a colossal bird. "Holy fuck, what is that?" Keith yells.

"I don't know. It has to have a wingspan of fifty feet. Carey, get in the fucking cabin"

As the bird gave off an ear-piercing shriek, the ground began to shake. Ridges started to rise up out of the dirt. They were moving towards Carey. Keith and Dean ran over to her, and grabbed her by the arm, but she didn't move. She was paralyzed by the bird circling above her, and didn't see the ridges in the ground forming around her.

"Carey, we've got to get the fuck out of here," Dean grabbed her arm but she still didn't move. Keith picked her up and put her over his shoulder. They ran into the cabin. When Keith put Carey down, she fell to the ground, still unable to speak. Her eyes wide open.

Dean stood by the door as the ridges, five or six of them, surrounded the cabin. He couldn't see the bird anymore, but could still hear its blistering shrieks. Keith stood next to him and watched the commotion outside.

"What the fuck is happening?" Dean said.

"I don't know."

"I think we're somewhere that we're not supposed to be."

XII

Highway 17

Sam was on his way back to his house after hiking on the mountain when he heard the sound of motorcycles coming up the road. It sounded like there were two of them. He was crossing the creek hidden on the forest's floor when they came into view. The one in front motioned Sam Coyote to follow him. Sam wasn't sure what to make of the gesture. The biker made the same motion to him again. The bikers never spoke, they never had time, perpetually on the highway.

Sam jumped on his own motorcycle. He followed the bikers until they came to Highway 17. A mile or two down the road, there was the blue and red hue from the emergency vehicles pulsating the sky. When he approached the scene, he could see that there were also several private vehicles scattered about too. A group of maybe two dozen bikers were all off their bikes standing in a line. Several men from the valley had formed their own line facing the bikers.

When Sam got out of his truck, Lola broke through the bikers and ran to him. She was crying and hysterical. "They killed him. The bastards killed him"

Sam tried to console her and calm her down. "What happened Lola?"

"They fucking killed him. They killed Victor." Victor was the guy that Lola's fiancé, the two of them had known each other since they were in high school.

"What happened?"

"Sheriff Jack and his deputy said that it was an accident, but that's not what happened. I know it. I saw the vision."

"Wait here." Sam walked past the line of bikers and saw Victor's body crumpled around a telephone post. His mangled bike still in the middle of the highway. An old Ford truck with a smashed in front grill was out in the field. A fat guy with a long beard was leaning against the truck holding a rag to his head to control the blood.

Sam Coyote went to talk to Matt the deputy sheriff who immediately pointed his gun at Sam. "Stay right there. This is an active accident investigation."

Sam kept walking towards the deputy. "Where is your boss?"

Matt took aim with his gun. "I told you to stop where you are at."

"Matt, put your gun down," Sheriff Jack yelled to his deputy.

Sam Coyote walked towards the sheriff. "What the hell happened here?"

"It looks like your boy from the Plane lost control of his motorcycle, crossed the center line and hit old Stanley head on, merely a tragic accident."

Sam looked back at the bikers who were all shaking their heads "no". A few of them had opened their jackets to make sure that their guns were visible. Lola was standing in front of them, "that's fucking bullshit Sam, the sheriff is lying to you. They killed him," she said.

Sam Coyote looked back at Jack. Over the sheriff's shoulder he could see a group of men from the valley stand at attention. Every single one of them was holding some type of rifle. "So, clear something up for me sheriff, if this is just a tragic accident, why did your friends have to show up so heavily armed? How did they get over here so fast?"

"I could ask the same of you Sam," he said nodding to the bikers behind him.

"You know how it is Jack, word travels faster on the Plane than it does through the valley. And you know that's a fact."

"Sam Coyote there's a lot of people in the valley who don't even believe some body from Plane can even die. Some of them even believe that the people from the Plane are immortal."

"Those are only stories people from the valley tell each other."

"No, Sam that's a lie. The old timers of the valley have plenty of stories about somebody from the Plane taking revenge on somebody from the valley for some petty reason."

"The people from the Plane know an accident when they see one. This doesn't look like an accident."

"There's a lot of people in the valley that are on edge right now after what happened in Las Vegas."

"Yeah, sheriff, you mentioned that to me before. You still haven't told me what makes you think that has anything to do with me or the Plane."

The bikers all started walking forward in unison toward Victor's body. The men from the valley started walking forward too. The sheriff turned around and put his hands up. "Put your guns down," he yelled to the men. "Go home."

Sam Coyote looked up the road to see a black hearse coming down the road. He pointed over to where Victor's body was. He held his arm around Lola while Victor was loaded into the vehicle. As the two of them walked back to Sam's truck, the sheriff yelled out, "it was an accident Sam Coyote, nothing more, nothing less."

"I'll tell everybody on the Plane that that is what you said. They can make up their own minds."

XIII

The Black Triangle

It had been a tradition for some time that Sam Coyote would go see Margaret at the UFO tower on the first Friday of every month, weather permitting. Margaret had built the UFO tower back in the seventies with idea that she would be able to study and document all of the strange lights and objects that streamed through the valley. She wrote a column for the newspaper, and had more than a few visits from the Air Force. It's a simple chain link structure and platform built over the café. She had no idea that the tower would eventually turn into the second biggest tourist attraction in valley, only the Sand Dunes drew more people. The alligator farm was a distant third.

"Sam Coyote," Margaret yelled down from the tower. "Your dinner is getting cold".

When he got to the top of the structure, there was one of Margaret's signature comfort food meals waiting for him, tonight it would be chicken enchiladas with rice and beans.

"Looks delicious," he said while giving Margaret a kiss on the cheek before sitting down.

"Well Sam Coyote, if tonight is anything like it's been the past few nights, we should be in for quite a show."

"There's been a lot of activity lately?"

"I've been in this valley for more than 65 years Sam Coyote, and I thought I had seen everything there was to see, but the past week has been the darndest thing. They've been visiting us like crazy. I've been half expecting them to try and make contact. One was so close, I thought it was going to land right over there".

"Why do you think that is Margaret? What's the occasion?"

"I'm not rightly sure Sam Coyote, but the helicopters have been thick as thieves too."

"It's been a long time since I've seen the helicopters."

"I had seen them every now and then, but now they must be on some kind of mission."

"What do you mean 'mission?"

"I don't know, but they're looking for something or someone".

Sam thought about Dimitrios but didn't say anything. He also thought about Sheriff Jack.

"It's your Plane Sam Coyote," Margaret continued. "There's something going on with the Plane. I'm an old lady, and for as long as I can remember the people of the Plane and the people of the valley have been able to coexist. You've gained maturity, give or take two or three incidents in the past, but it feels like something about the Plane has changed. There's a tension to it that the valley people can feel."

"Well, there's – "

"Look over there!" Margaret stood up and pointed to the southwest sky. A giant black triangle hovering, it's edges a dull green light making it visible in the night sky. A light hum filled the air. "That's a big one. You don't see the triangles often. Usually, it's the blue or red orbs."

Sam pointed to the north. "There's another one over there."

"See Coyote, there's something in the sky every single night lately."

As fast as the triangles had appeared, they were gone. From over the sand dunes, six separate small lights appeared on the horizon. Three of the lights moved to the southwest where the first triangle had been, the other three went to the north.

"There's the helicopters," Margaret said.

"It's not 'my Plane', and why do you think it us? The people who live on the Plane, are just like the people from the valley, we all bleed just the same. The only real difference is that we are little more aware of what is going on around us. They've been seeing lights in the sky over this valley for centuries. There was a Spanish guy who wrote about seeing them in his journal in 1777."

"That's true, but Sam Coyote, you have to understand that the Plane and the valley are not mutually exclusive, they are symbiotic, you can't have one without the other. When there is turbulence in the valley, it affects the Plane. When something is amiss on the Plane it is felt in the valley."

"There was a man who showed up at my place last week. He says his name is Dimitrios. He's staying over at the Drive-In Inn in Monte Vista. Nobody seems to know what to make of him. On the surface, he appears to be a nice enough guy, but there's an edge to him that is hard to define. An energy"

"Ariel was here today. You know how much she likes my vortex garden. She sat down there for hours and meditated. When she was done, she came into the café for tea and we chatted for a while. She didn't say anything about a man, but she mentioned some hikers. She seemed kind of worried about them"

"I've been meaning to go see her for some time now, just haven't had the chance."

"It's funny that you say that Sam Coyote, Ariel told me that if I see you, I am supposed to tell you to go see her."

XIV

Something has Arrived

Ariel's Intersection Spiritual Center in Crestone is an architectural anomaly. The shape is a cross between a medieval castle and a Hindu temple, but it is all fashioned out of stucco covered adobe. It sits on the highest hill in town, with the Sangre De Cristo Mountains as a backdrop. Specifically designed at an angle to achieve maximum sunlight from dawn until dusk.

Sam walked into the center; it was always open and had never had locks on the doors. An old dog hobbled his way over and sniffed Sam's hand. As he petted the dog it whimpered.

"He's dying." Sam turned around to see Ariel. "It's lymphoma," she says.

"He's always been a good dog".

"Yes, he has Sam. What brings you here today?"

"Margaret was saying that you wanted to talk to me."

"I'm going to get straight to the point. I don't like the feelings that I have been getting lately."

"I don't understand. What do you mean?" Sam knew what she talking about, but didn't let on.

"The Plane, this Plane of existence that we are all sharing, this valley that has been so harmonious for so long, feels like it is being corrupted."

"Ariel, you're not the only one that feels it. It's not just the Plane people either. The valley people seem a little on edge too."

"Sam, I was drawn to this place long, long ago. I've been almost everywhere and everywhen. I didn't arbitrarily get to this Plane. It grabbed me the way a Venus fly trap grabs its prey. It became my cocoon, after an eternity of searching I found a place where my soul could be nurtured and flourish. I've never experienced that on any other Plane. There is such a feeling of belonging."

"I've known you for a long time Ariel. You have been a love of mine for as long as I can remember. You are not one to tolerate any irritation in your realm. I've seen what can happen with my own eyes"

"I meditate at dawn every morning, and then again at dusk. I let the peace of this place swaddle me. It is my greatest comfort. Last night, for the first time, my meditation was disturbed."

"By what?"

"Screams."

"Who was screaming?"

"I don't know. There were three voices. Somewhere out in the wilderness. It felt like by the sand dunes. Sam, these were screams of sheer terror, like nothing I have ever experienced here before. My thoughts and dreams were invaded."

"I have to confess, that's not at all what I was expecting you to say."

"Oh no, what were you expecting?"

"I assume you know about the guy showing up at my place."

"I had a vision. I've heard noises"

"His name is Dimitrios. He showed up at my place covered in blood. He seemed completely lost. He told me that he had no memory of how he got here. But I don't think he is lost at all. There is some purpose for him being here. It might be for me."

"There are certain souls that are drawn to this place simply for its duality. It's the perfect intersection of space and time. The mountains on each side of the valley have a lot to do with it. To the east you the Sangre DeCristo range and to the west are the San Juan's. They are completely different ranges with unique personalities but they are symbiotic enough to create this perfect valley. But the mountains are symbolic, they may as well be the Pacific and Atlantic oceans.

"I love you Ariel, but I wish you would say what you mean."

She smiled. "Think about it Sam, this valley is much like a beach. The ocean represents the unknown. The beach represents the willingness to walk into it."

Sam rolled his eyes. "Ariel, you were just saying that you didn't want the unknown on this Plane."

"You misunderstood me. That's not what I said at all. The unknown is healthy. It begs for us to explore it, to further our ultimate knowledge. No, what has come to the valley isn't the unknown. This is something completely different. There is a different Plane intersecting with this one now and there are some bad inhabitants of this new Plane. There's a tension in the air."

"This Dimitrios guy, maybe he's part of that Plane."

"That's possible. Lilith hasn't been the greatest addition either."

"The sheriff pulled me over the other day. In a way, he asked me about the guy without knowing about him. For being such a cocksucker, Jack can be surprisingly intuitive."

"That is odd."

"I don't know for sure, or even why, but I think Dimitrios and I have crossed paths in the past. I'm not even sure he knows that yet."

"This situation needs to be handled. On the surface, this may not seem like a big deal, this is an existential crisis with ramifications that cannot be calculated"

XV

The Nazi

"I recognize you".

Dimitrios woke up at the Drive In Inn. He didn't know why.

"I recognize you". He heard the voice again. Still in bed, Dimitrios saw some light through the drapes.

"I recognize you". Dimitrios got out of bed. He opened the curtains and saw himself on the drive-screen. He was bartending at the usual place. He looked around to see who it was that recognized him.

There at the bar was a guy, probably in his mid-twenties, with thick glasses, a pear-shaped body. His teeth were stained a glossy brown, and his hair was matted. His tee-shirt read, "MY PERFECT DAY. Wake up. Play video games. Eat Breakfast. Play video games. Eat lunch. Play video games. Eat lunch. Play video games. Have a snack. Play video games. Eat dinner. Play video games. Have a snack. Play video games. Have another snack. Play video games. Go to sleep." Dimitrios could still remember the guy's body odor.

"Do recognize me?"

Dimitrios looked at the guy. "No".

"Are you sure?"

"Yeah, I'm sure. Can I get you something to drink?"

"My name is Richie".

"Nice to meet you Richie," Dimitrios said. "Can I get you something to drink?"

"I like Mountain Dew".

"We don't have that here. I think they have it at the snack bar over by the elevators".

"Do they have Doritos too?"

"I honestly don't know."

"Don't you recognize me? I'm Richie."

"I'm sorry Richie. I don't recall ever meeting you before."

"Is your name Dimitrios?"

"Yes".

"You're a liberal piece of shit, aren't you Dimitrios? You're the guy that thinks he's so much smarter than everybody. Oooooh, you're so much more enlightened than the rest of us. An elitist"

"I'm sorry. What?" Instead of reacting, he had to remind himself that was on the job.

"You're that libtard fuck that preaches all of your communist bullshit on the internet."

Dimitrios studied Richie's face for a moment. "Oh yeah, you're the internet troll. It's a pleasure to meet you. Can I get you something to drink?"

"I'm not a troll. I'm a patriot. I'm a Christian. I care about this country. I want this country to be great again. You want babies to ripped from their mother's wombs." Richie's voice got louder.

"Sir," Dimitrios tried to calm Richie. "Is there something I can get for you?"

"I wouldn't give you one dime of my money."

"Can I ask you why you are here then?"

"You do know the scope of the conference that is going on here?"

"My manager said something about it, but I didn't pay much attention. I just do my job."

"Well, Dimitrios, I helped put this conference together, along with my father. That's the kind of pull that I have. When history tells the story of our time, this gathering will be written about as one of the most important gatherings in the history of the United States of America. It will mark the day that the citizens of this great country rose up to take it back from the illegal immigrants, gays, baby killers, and all of you left wing radicals that are trying to destroy this country and turned it into some shithole."

Dimitrios smirked. "Is this because I called you a 'Nazi' online?"

"Oh, no sir. I where that label as a badge of honor." Richie pulled the shirt down over his shoulder to show off a swastika tattoo.

"Richie, I'm trying to do my job, so if you don't want something to drink, I have other customers to take care of."

"I organized this conference," Richie told Dimitrios. "I specifically chose this place because I saw on your profile that you worked here, and I figured that if a traitor like you worked here, there were probably others too. I wanted to parade it in front of your face."

"Well thank you, this is one of the finest casinos around. We appreciate your patronage." It took a moment for Dimitrios to comprehend how disturbing Richie's words were.

"You are what is wrong with this country, you and your liberal fucking views. I'm going to make sure that every true American at this freedom conference comes specifically to this bar when you are working to expose you for who you are."

"Again, Richie, I thank you for your patronage to this fine casino. I appreciate you steering tips in my direction. If you are looking for Mountain Dew, Doritos, and video games I would suggest you talk to the concierge about the children's section of the casino."

"Fuck you. I am not a child. I'm here to change the face of the country. To expose liberals like you as the threat that you are. If you disrespect me again, I will talk to your manager. This conference is spending a lot of money here."

"I can get my manager now if you would like."

"Dimitrios, I'm going to make your life a living hell."

"Richie, can't you have your civil war without me? It's not my fault that you and your little incel friends can't get laid"

The images on the drive-in screen abruptly faded away. Dimitrios could see a lone coyote walking among the old speaker poles.

XVI

Our Place

Dimitrios was suspicious of the knock on the big wooden door because that wasn't something that had happened before. He hesitated before turning the lever, but then came three more knocks. He looked around the kitchen. There was a knife on the counter that he grabbed. He opened the door with his left hand, the knife in his right. Through the crack in the door, he saw a fat guy with a big smile on his face. "Are you Dimitrios?" the fat guy said.

"Yes," Dimitrios answered.

"I'm Eugene, I heard you were new on the Plane."

"I am, thank you. What do you mean 'Plane?'"

"We'll talk about that as it comes up. Has anybody shown you around?"

"Not really."

"Come out. Let's go have a drink. You do drink, don't you?"

"A strong drink sounds fantastic, but can I ask why you knocked on this door? Why not the front door?"

"The front door?"

Dimitrios pointed to the door on the other side of the room. "Wow," Eugene said. "I had no idea that there were other doors to this place. I thought there were only the tunnel doors."

Dimitrios stepped out into the stone wall tunnel, and looked around. "Where does this all lead? I wanted to explore it, but I figured I was lost enough already"

Eugene laughed. "These tunnels lead you everywhere you need to go. You can be above ground, and it will get you around the valley, but it's the tunnel underneath the valley that gets you around the Plane."

"Why do you keep saying 'Plane?"

"I'm sorry," Eugene said. "I keep forgetting that you are new here. There are people here that could explain this place better to you than I ever could. It feels small, but there are thousands of us here."

"Is one of those people Sam Coyote?"

"Oh yeah, he's certainly one of them."

"I met him my first day here. I don't know what to make of him."

"Sam's a good guy, once you get to know him. I had a hell of a time going fishing with him the other morning. Let's go have a drink."

"I don't think I have any money."

Eugene laughed so hard he had to drop to one knee. "Goddamn boy, you have no idea where you are, do you? You don't need money here. The concept of money is what makes the valley folk the way that they are"

"I don't need money?

"Boy, you are greener than anybody that has ever been here. I like that. Come on. Are you playing me Dimitrios?" Eugene studied him. "No, that's not it. You had some kind of epiphany. What happened to you?"

"I had a strange night recently. I wasn't myself anymore"

Eugene and Dimitrios walked through the catacomb of tunnels, and as they walked Eugene pointed out to Dimitrios the significances of all of the tunnels and where they led. They finally came to a tunnel that was lit up by a neon walkway.

"Some people use Tunnel Time, but I don't."

"Tunnel Time?"

"Somebody else will have to explain that to you too."

"This is our place," Eugene said pointing the way down the tunnel.

The two men walked through a door that was identical to the one that led into Dimitrios' motel room. But it, was a smoke-filled room with music booming off of the ceiling. The twenty or so people that were in the place were all dancing.

Eugene and Dimitrios walked over and sat at the bar. Lilith walked over to them. "Eugene, it's been a while. It's like I haven't seen you since last night."

"I don't remember being here last night."

"I didn't think you would."

"Last night got a little rough."

"So, who's your friend Eugene?"

"This is Dimitrios. He's new around here."

Lilith studied Dimitrios for a while. "I've heard about you and now we finally meet. You are the guy that showed up at Sam's place the other day."

"Yeah, that would be me. I don't know how I ended up there, I just did."

Lilith looked at Dimitrios, then over at Eugene. "I call bullshit on that, what do you think?"

Eugene raised his eyebrows but didn't say anything.

"I like where I am," Dimitrios said. "I don't know why, but I do. It feels like the right place to be."

Lilith fixated her eyes on Dimitrios. "You're pretty hot."

"Thank you."

"Do you like hot springs Dimitrios?"

"I guess. I didn't even know there were any hot springs here."

"I own it. It's kind of the hot place to be on the Plane."

"Why does everybody keep calling this place a Plane?"

Lilith looked at Eugene. "He doesn't know?" she said.

Eugene shook his head. "No. Not that I can tell."

"Dimitrios," Lilith said. "I've been expecting you. There's a tunnel not too far from here. You need to come talk to me."

Eugene tapped Dimitrios on the leg, and whispered into his ear. "Before you go talk to her, you need to go talk to Lee."

XVII

The Difference

When Dimitrios woke up in the morning he looked over on the nightstand and saw the keys to his truck. It probably didn't make any sense to even guess how they got there. He looked out the window and the truck parked right there. Sometimes it's better not to ask why things are the way they are.

After a quick shower, Dimitrios was behind the wheel. He was finally going to get to explore the San Luis Valley from above the ground instead by the tunnels underneath it. After a trip through the LaGarita Mountains, he drove to Alamosa. There were little shops and restaurants on Main Street that made him think of a Norman Rockwell painting. Driving by Adams State College, he ogled all of the little co-eds. It wasn't that big of town, so he saw most of it pretty quick and soon became bored.

He ended up at an old grey stone building with two huge wood carved statues out in front. One was an old cigar store Indian. He wasn't sure what the other one was, but he guessed that it was some type of alien. Above the door was a wooden sign, "San Luis Historical Society and Café". It seemed like a good way to kill some time.

An old man was there to greet him. Lee had been born in Alamosa, and for a man of his age, he appeared to be in good shape. He had a full head of curly hair that still hadn't gone completely grey. "Welcome to San Luis Historical Society and Café," he said to Dimitrios extending his hand.

"Hello." Dimitrios shook Lee's hand.

"What brings you in here today?"

"Oh, I'm stayin up in Monte Vista and I was out sightseeing and saw the place. It seemed interesting so I thought I would stop in."

"Anything in particular you wanted to know about the San Luis Valley?"

"I've never been here. I don't know anything at all about it".

"Oh, where are my manners? My name is Lee."

"Dimitrios".

"Where you from Dimitrios?"

"Las Vegas".

"Do you have relatives here?

"No, I was on a road trip to nowhere and I ended up here".

"Well, Dimitrios, you ended up in a special place. I've lived here all my life. The Mrs. and I have been married for sixty years. Our great-grandchildren live just down the road in Fort Garland. It's the most unique place on Earth. I've been all over the world in my 84 years on this planet, and I can guarantee that there is no place like it. I am the descendant of a great Ute warrior"

"I've had some interesting experiences while I've been here".

"Experiences? What kind of experiences?"

"You know," Dimitrios sighed. "Experiences".

Lee sensed that the visitor did not want to be pressed. "This valley is known for many things. They got special potatoes grown where your stayin, in Monte Vista. Hell, you can keep Idaho potatoes. They aren't worth the spit used to shine them compared to Monte Vista potatoes. I'll bet that if you're from Las Vegas you're probably a boxing fan."

"I've seen some great fights on the strip. Legendary fights"

"A few miles south of here is a town called Manassa. Old turn of the century mining town, and hometown of Jack Dempsey. The Manassa Mauler, Jack Dempsey. The greatest heavyweight champion of all time. The family cabin is still standing. There's a statue of the champ out front."

Dimitrios smiled at Lee's enthusiasm. "I'll have to go check that out sometime".

"Would you like something to eat?"

"No, I should get going. I thought I would pop my head in and see what the place looked like, but I would like to come back another time and get a chance to look around".

"That would be nice Dimitrios. The place hardly ever closes. I can tell you about the history of the valley. There have been 12 native American Indian tribes that have called valley home at one time or another. We're called the UFO capital of the world. There's even a UFO watchtower up north, near Hooper. And maybe in the middle of lunch I'll tell you about all of the cattle mutilations in this area." Lee winked at Dimitrios.

"Cattle mutilations?"

"Like I said, over lunch another time."

Dimitrios laughed and turned to walk out the door. "Next time," Lee said. "I'll tell you how to tell the difference between a valley person and Plane person."

Dimitrios stopped in his tracks. "Lee, I keep hearing the term 'Plane' and 'valley'. I don't know what it all means"

Lee shook his head. "It's something you will have study for yourself, but I can give you a short answer. The people of the Plane are what one might called old souls. They have lived many lives before; they are adept at navigating the universe. The people of the valley are newer souls, they are still trying to figure out what the world is all about. That's the simplest way I can explain it"

XVIII

Stand Now

There was the sound of applause. "Good evening. I am Congressman Longstreet." There was even louder applause, and yelling and screaming.

Dimitrios sat straight up in his bed from deep sleep at the Drive-In Inn. At first, he thought that he had a nightmare, but he kept hearing the applause. The familiar light penetrating the seam in the drapes. He got out of bed and parted the cloth. Once again, there were visions on the drive-in theater's screen. There hadn't been a car in front of that screen for at least 25 years.

There was becoming a theme to the visions. He had his bartender uniform on, the one of three that the casino had given him. On most nights, he worked the bar by the craps tables, but that night there was a popular speaker at the convention going on so they put him at temporary bar in the auditorium. With protesters out front, he wondered if management regretted booking the convention.

The applause died down. "Good evening. I am Congressman Longstreet. I am here tonight to tell you that this country is headed for the greatest threat it has ever faced, we are headed for catastrophe...."

"Who is this guy?" Dimitrios asked the other bartender.

"It's some kind of patriot convention," he said using air quotes.

"I don't know why they took me off the bar to do this."

"Surprisingly, I made pretty good money last night," the bartender said.

"……if we don't act fast, the congressman continued his speech, "they are trying to kill us off, they are trying to kill off the white man, they think that we are the enemies…."

"Geez, I can't believe he just said that," Dimitrios laughed.

"You should have heard the guy last night, going on and on about abortion, and guns, and homosexual agendas, the guy was a piece of work, but look at the audience. They can't get enough. They eat it up"

Dimitrios looked around the audience. He couldn't wait for the shift to be over.

The images on the screen morphed to the next night when he was at his usual bar by the craps tables. It was a slower night. At a slot machine to the right of the bar was a guy who looked familiar to Dimitrios. He was small in stature, with a bad combover and bright blue eyes that were slightly crossed. Dimitrios studied him, but couldn't place him. He went off to help his customers.

When there was moment of peace at the bar, Dimitrios noticed the man at the slot machine again. He was probably in his mid-sixties and judging by the way he was dressed, probably from somewhere in the Midwest. As he tried to place him, two elderly men approached him.

"That was a hell of a speech you gave last night Congressman Longstreet'"

The congressman must have celebrated his speech pretty good the night before, in fact, he may have never stopped. He looked like he was in rough shape.

"Asshole," Dimitrios mumbled under his breath and went back to work.

About 15 minutes later, Dimitrios sensed a customer rushing to his bar. He looked over to see the congressman. "I'll be right with you."

As Dimitrios approached he could tell that congressman could barely stand up. "What can I get you?"

"Double crown on the rocks," the congressman said with a slight slur.

"That's top shelf stuff."

Dimitrios handed him the drink. "Are you a white man?" the congressman asked.

"Excuse me?"

"Are you a white man?" The congressman's voice grew angry, he was slurring his words.

"What you see is what you get."

"You can't be a white man, because if you were, you would be madder than hell right now!"

"Enjoy your drink sir, I have other customers to take care of."

"You'd be angry right now," the congressman shouted as Dimitrios walked away. "You had better get angry boy, because when the black man and the brown man band together and rise up against the white man, it's your sissy ass liberals that are going to come running to the patriots for protection, but we're not going to help you. If you don't stand with the patriots now, the patriots won't stand with you when you need them. The white man must concentrate on breeding his women"

XIX

They Followed Me

Jack watched as the eight ball went into the corner pocket. He was still in uniform when he went and grabbed the two twenties sitting on the rail of the table. "Good game sheriff," the loser said as he walked back to the booth by the window. Jack nodded his head and went over and sat at the bar.

"You going to have another one sheriff?" the bartender, a skinny young girl wearing too much makeup to cover the scars she had picked while doing meth, asked.

"Yeah, one more. Let's make it a shot of Fireball this time. And do I owe you anything?"

The bartender rolled her eyes. "No sheriff." He smiled at her, slammed the shot and walked out to the patrol vehicle. He looked at the old Ford Bronco and thought about what a cheap county he was working in, but at least it was 100% made in America. The state troopers were all driving Dodge Chargers, but they had some Japanese parts he heard.

He drove the five miles down highway 160 until he got to the dirt road that would take him home. Once he was off the highway, he pulled over and opened up the center console. There was a plastic bag that had around an ounce of mushrooms in it. He had confiscated them from some kids driving through from California. The kids actually had four ounces of the psychedelic spores on them, but Jack knew that three ounces would be enough to charge them, so no sense in letting the rest of them go to waste. He grabbed a handful and shoved them in his mouth and started driving again.

Sheriff Jack pulled into the driveway and sat there for a minute. This was the part of the day that he hated the most. Home was a double-wide trailer among the sagebrush with its paint peeling and the rotting wood steps leading into it. He looked around, there wasn't another house or car in sight. Just the way he liked it. There was a jackrabbit sitting below the bedroom window. He reached for his gun, but got bored by the idea. The front door of the trailer and made him wish that the mushrooms would kick in faster, but he walked in anyway.

His wife Amber came over and give him one of her emotionless hugs and a fake kiss. "You won't believe what happened to me. I was driving home from the grocery store today, and this pickup full of dirty Mexicans pulled up next to me. They started telling me how fine I was and asked if I wanted to come with them. I told them to fuck off, and that I didn't do wetbacks. I don't know if they were legal or not."

"They're all illegal," Jack said. "They're always saying to me that their kind was on this land way before the white man ever was. I say to them, 'Well we won the war motherfuckers. This is our land now. Your land is on the other side of the river, so get back on over there."

"I wish everybody would wake the fuck up. We are being invaded, but it will be patriots like us that will win this war. I thought those savages were going rape me and make me do whatever they wanted. I wouldn't have any choice but to submit to whatever they wanted."

Jack stared at his wife for a moment, puzzled by what she had said. "Speaking of the patriots, I heard over the radio today that they think they might know who did the shooting in Las Vegas, but they have no idea where he is. Don't even know where to look. They haven't put out a name or picture, so nobody knows what to look for. They're covering this up"

"You know it had to be a wetback."

"I don't think so, they're not smart enough. I'm guessing it was one of their sympathizers. It was a traitor. A traitor not only to his country, but to his own kind. That's the worst kind of traitor."

"I hope the patriots get to him before law enforcement does."

"Whoever it is better hope law enforcement gets to him before the patriots do. That will be a special kind of torture. But don't worry, there are a lot of patriots that are cops."

"I was afraid that truck full of Mexicans was going to rape me today. They're such animals. They followed me for a while down the highway. I thought for sure that they were going to rape me."

Jack stared at Amber. He felt a sense of anger, but he couldn't express it. The mushrooms were starting to kick in. He could only see trails of her face as she spoke. She rubbed his dick. That is all he could remember.

"I'm telling you Jack, it's time for drastic measures."

When the mushrooms kicked, Jack knew the dragons

were outside the door.

XX

The Serpent and the Egg

Lola walked around that shed, past the riding circle, and straight towards the corrals. The horse sensed that she was coming. He started raring and stood on his hind legs and held it there for several seconds before dropping down and making quick gallops around his pen. "Are you excited to see me Phantom?" Lola called out. Once again, the horse held a pose on his back feet.

She couldn't help but admire Phantom, he was a majestic equine specimen. Bigger and leaner than most horses, muscular build, he could be an intimidating sight. A flawless jet-black coat covered him the hoofs up, head to tail. With one exception, his face. There was a perfect white square that started above his eyes and covered his nose and mouth. He was still a young colt, probably had some thoroughbred in him, and could become unruly for other people that tried to handle him, but never around Lola. He was perfectly calm with her. Always had been, she watched him being born.

"Saddle him up," Eugene yelled from the cabin.

"Good morning pops"

"Hold on. Let me get dressed. You get them ready and I'll be out in a little bit."

About an hour later, twenty minutes into the ride, Lola asked Eugene where they were riding, she didn't recognize the trail.

"I've only taken a couple of other people ever. I usually keep it for my own little place, only go there when it calls me. It's been whispering in my ear later lately. I figured you were the perfect person to take. You're pretty much a granddaughter to me."

Lola looked at Eugene for a long while. She couldn't decide whether he was joking or not. "Well thank you Pops. That's nice of you."

"Well, thing with you and Sam, and me and Sam. That's kinda the way it feels to me."

"Awe, I love you Pops.

They rode in silence for several minutes. "So," Lola said. "You never said where we were riding too."

"It's not something that can be adequately expressed by words. You just have to see it."

"Fair enough."

It was one of the tougher rides that Eugene had taken

Lola on, but Phantom handled the terrain perfectly. Over the

crest of the hill, Lola started noticing stone walls, they seemed

to be going in every which direction. For the first time ever,

Lola could sense some kind of tension about Phantom. "What

is this place?"

"They call them the stone snakes. They have another

mystical name for them, but I can never pronounce it."

Lola got off of Phantom and started walking around

the walls. The horse galloped away from the rows of stone.

"Why are they here Pops?"

"Nobody knows."

"What are they supposed to keep in? Or keep out?"

"That's the funny thing. There is no enclosure. They're

free flowing."

Lola walked up closer to one of the walls. "So,

somebody laid all of these stones by hand, and nobody

knows why?"

"Nope. I've read that some people think it was a type of drainage system, and there are others think it was kind of a hunting trap. Neither one of those things seemed to make sense to me."

"What do you think it is?"

"In all the years of coming up here I still can't quite put my finger on exactly what it is, but there is one thing I'm sure of, it's a powerful place. There is a power here like I've never experienced before. You know how I told you how I would only come here when it called me to?"

"Sure, Pops."

"When it calls me, it comes as a vision, like a still photograph of a location somewhere within the walls. The vision has been the never been the same, not once."

"What have you been seeing lately?

Eugene motioned at Lola to follow him. They walked to the end of one the rows of stone. He pointed to a carving on a big stone. Lola studied it for a while. "Is it an egg in a snake's mouth?"

He laughed. "That's what I thought at first too. No, it's not an egg, it's the sun. If you talked to any of the Indians that come through here every now and then. They'll tell you that a serpent is holding the sun in its mouth, and when the serpent releases the sun it will be brand new world."

Lola looked at him. She nodded that she understood.

"You feel it," he said. "It feels like there's a pretty big serpent holding the valley in its mouth. I have a feeling that it is going to be you that has to release the sun."

XXI

Who's Who

Lilith felt the sheets move. She looked to her right and smiled. She remembered that he said he had just turned 21. He wanted to spend his birthday with his girlfriend at the hot springs. At the end of the weekend, he was going to propose to his girlfriend. Lilith licked her lips as she looked at his naked body. He was flawless, she thought. Tall and lean, with very little body fat. It seemed like his muscles were highlighted in the copper hue of the rising sun. She had had bigger dicks, but this kid knew how to use it.

She rolled over to her left. The guy's girlfriend, or soon to be fiancé, was equally impressive. Lilith was tempted to kiss her, but didn't want to wake her up. The girl was a petite thing. Big breasts with puffy nipples. Her body sporadically covered with tattoos. It was hard to believe that she was only 18 and about to be somebody's wife. Age is just a number, Lilith thought to herself. That girl is wise and erotic beyond her years.

There was a knock at the door, that gradually turned into banging. Lilith didn't bother to put on any clothes before she opened the door. It was Ariel, and Lilith sensed that she was upset about something.

"Good morning, Lilith."

"Ariel! Perfect timing. Come in. We should probably keep it to a whisper. I have the most adorable couple asleep up in my bed."

"I can't stay, I...."

"Yeah, well I don't want to stand here naked here at the door."

Lilith grabbed Ariel by the hand and lead her to a little patio area out by the hot springs. They both sat down on the couch. "I can wait while you go put a robe on."

"I'm fine Arial. You know why I said it was perfect timing that you were here?"

"Why is that?"

"Before you knocked, I was looking at that naked girl's body and thinking about how good we fucked each other last night. I was getting so horny, but I didn't want to wake her up. Then you knocked. See, perfect timing. You want to take off that pretty little dress and get in the water and a play around. I've had my eye on you since I arrived here."

"That's why I'm here."

Lilith leaned in to kiss Ariel. "Oh baby, get naked, I'll make you cum like you've never came before."

Ariel used her palm to push back. "That's not the part that I was talking about. I was talking about the part about you buying this place. You don't understand it."

"I understand perfectly. I was drawn here. I can't explain it. This place was a magnet for me. I have a feeling more people will be arriving soon"

"Do you know where you are?"

Lilith smiled. "I know exactly where I'm at, and I'm not going anywhere soon. This place needs to be where people come to loosen up."

"Now, I don't think you do. This is Crestone. Crestone, Colorado. It's is one of the most spiritual places anywhere and anytime. Some say it is the center of the universe. There is not a faith anywhere that isn't represented by somebody living here or in the hills."

"I'm not sure that I'm getting your point Ariel. Or care. This has nothing to do with me"

"Lilith, this is a community. We, also, have been drawn to this place by our experiences in other places. We recognize that this is the center of it all. We are all connected by that desire to grow. To attaining the highest powers of this existence."

"Just say what you mean Ariel. You don't have to dance around it with that cult talk."

"The people who owned the hot springs before you knew the psychoactive powers of that water. They used it to bring knowledge and wisdom to those who sat in its warmth. They used it to help their fellow souls along in the journey."

"I'm sorry Ariel, that was then, this is now. Each of us has our own path"

"Enlightenment means different things to different people. I'm going to be blunt with you Lilith, the powers of the water in these springs possess the ability to change a soul. That's what these waters are for. To heal and to inspire. You don't use the waters for that though, you use them as a source of personal debauchery. It used to be that we could hear your orgies on a Friday or Saturday night. Then it started happening every night, then during the day. Now it's nonstop sex all the time."

"All the more reason to get a room and come lighten up and have some fun. Of course, you and I would have the whole hot spring to ourselves right now."

"No thank you Lilith. It would be nice if you got to know who some of your neighbors. That way you could figure out who's who around here.

"Oh, believe me, I'm getting to know a lot of them."

XXII

Every Trail has to Lead Somewhere

"The ground is pretty torn up, but it looks like whatever was out there is gone," Dean said to Carey and Keith.

"They're not gone." Carey's voice was panicked.

"We can't just wait here. Nobody knows where we are," Keith said. "We've been here for two days. We need water"

"I'm not fucking going out there!"

"Carey, god damn, we're running out of fucking supplies," Keith pleaded. "We can't stay here. There's no rescue party coming. Nobody will miss us for at least a week. We have got to leave."

Dean walked over to Carey until he was eye level with her. "Here's what we'll do. I have a whistle in my backpack. I'll go out there and take a look around. I'll see what the trail looks like. If everything looks cool, I'll blow the whistle, and then you two come up and meet me. I'll scout ahead again, and blow the whistle again. We'll keep doing that until we get back to the car."

Keith and Carey watched as Dean walked through the small meadow and into the trees. "How long did he say he would be before he was going to blow the whistle?" Carey asked.

"He didn't say. He said he was going look around. Knowing Dean, it might be a while."

As they stood at the door, Keith ran his arm down Carey's back. "Are you okay?" He asked.

She didn't say anything. She looked at Keith as if she were going to cry. "It's okay," he pulled her closer into him. "I know what would relax both of us." Keith started kissing Carey's neck.

"Are you fucking crazy? What the fuck is wrong with you?" Carey went from tearful to rage-filled in a split second.

Before Keith could say anything, they heard the whistle. "Let's go." Carey grabbed her backpack and started walking to the trail.

"Hold on Carey, I've got to get my shit together."

Carey hadn't heard him. He looked out the door, she was nowhere to be seen. "Carey, wait up," he yelled into the forest, and started running down the trail.

As Carey walked, she didn't remember the foliage being so thick. She remembered a mostly clear path. She certainly didn't remember pushing branches away from her face. She turned a full circle looking around. There was no trail to be seen. So badly, she wanted to scream and go into a panicked fetal ball. She knew couldn't, she had to be still and listen for the whistle. There was a sound straight ahead, like a humming sound. She pushed forward until she came to a clearing.

The humming that she heard, was from the engine of a car. It was odd she thought. The car was beautiful. It looked brand new, though Carey thought that it must have been made in the thirties. It was hard to reconcile the sight in her mind. She had done all of the research for the hiking trip, and she knew there wasn't supposed to be a road there. It did occur to her that maybe she was more lost than she realized. She waved to the car. The back door of the car opened, and out stepped a tall, dark young man in a stylish suit.

"I'm lost," Carey yelled out. "Can you give me a lift to the main road?" The man motioned for her to come.

Keith was on a trail. He didn't know if it was the right trail, he never heard the whistle and Carey wasn't answering him. It made sense to him that every trail has to lead somewhere. The sun was about to be entirely engulfed by the San Juan Mountains. He started looking for a place to camp for the night. Dean was the one who had the tent, so he would be sleeping under the stars. The fear was long gone, but he was exhausted and sleep came easily for Keith.

He didn't know what time it was when the sound of music woke him up, it was faint but Keith could still hear it. The moonless sky was impossibly black save for one star. He got out of his sleeping bag and looked around. He fumbled through trees until there was a light. It had a reddish hue. There was a woman dressed in a red evening gown. She knew he was there, and motioned him to come to her. He paused, but didn't stop long to consider the situation. As he approached, she slid the straps of gown off. Keith approached her and immediately started kissing her and pinching her nipples. She reached down and undid Keith's shorts. He got down on his knees and pulled the dress off her hips. A goat hoof kicked him square in the teeth.

XXIII

The Author

It was a Monday, not many tourists in the casino, just convention goers. Dimitrios didn't like them all that much, and couldn't wait for the gathering to end. They seemed to live in a fantasy land. Still, they tipped okay. He had heard that they were going to be there all week.

He looked around the casino, the dealers were all standing around their tables waiting for some suckers to play their game. All but two of the drinks that Dimitrios had poured had been for cocktail waitresses serving old people playing the slot machines, and even those were quieter than usual. He noticed that most of the people walking around that night held the same white book. It made Dimitrios curious, but not curious enough to ask somebody what the book was.

There was a rush to the bar after a book signing let out. People had set the book next to their drinks. On the cover was an attractive woman with blonde hair that went down to her waist. She had one foot up on a clear bench so that her shapely legs were the focal point of the cover. Across the bottom of the cover it read, "How the Left became the Mortal Enemy of Common Decency – It's time to make America a Christian Nation Once Again" by Eleanor Prudhomme.

Most the clientele that night were middle aged men, who had one, maybe two beers and went back to their rooms. A few of the younger guys, almost all of them wearing camouflage, stuck around to gamble a bit at the cheap tables. And just fast as it got busy, it was dead again. The pit boss started shutting down all of the tables until there was only one for each game. Dimitrios looked at his watch. It was going to be a long six hours.

At around midnight a swirl of activity came through the casino entrance. There were probably 15-20 people coming in at once. They walked around the tables, but didn't seem interested in gambling. Dimitrios' bar was the only one that was still open at that hour so most of the people sat there. As he scrambled to take orders and pour drinks, he recognized one of the people. The long blonde hair. The lady from the cover of the book. Eleanor Prudhomme.

"What can I get you to drink?" Dimitrios asked her.

"I'll have blue martini." Her voice was deep.

"We had a nice draw tonight, Eleanor," Dimitrios overheard part of what someone in her entourage said to her. "I was nervous about booking you on a Monday night, but that was a great idea to only sign books that they had to purchase on site. I don't have the final numbers, but I know we cleaned up there."

"Honey," Eleanor said, "whenever there's one of these types of conventions anywhere, you can book me any night you want. Mondays might even be better, because all of their wives will be tired from the weekend, so all of these horny old guys can buy one of my books and I let them look down my shirt while I sign it for them."

"I think there's something in the South next month."

"There's always something going on in the south," Eleanor laughed. "The problem is there is no money to be made in the south. They're not going to pay $35 a pop for a book they probably won't be able to read so they can see the tops of my tits. Fuck that. Fuck the South unless it's a huge upfront fee. That's the only way you can make the dollars there, you sure the fuck aren't going to make a dime selling books. They're the only ones that believe this is real, nobody let them in on the joke"

Dimitrios sat the blue martini down in front of her, "There you go ma'am, that will $19.50."

The author looked at the woman who had been speaking. The woman handed Dimitrios a credit card. "These drink prices are a bigger joke than this convention is"

When Dimitrios returned with the credit card slip, Eleanor Prudhomme was gone. The woman handed Dimitrios a small envelope. "She wants you call her when you get off."

XXIV

The Stations

"It's beautiful, "Lola said.

Margaret smiled at her. Yes, it is. It's called 'La Mesa de la Piedad y de la Misericorida'. That's Spanish for 'The Hill of Piety and Mercy'. Since I first came here as a little girl, I've loved the power of this place. I can feel Jesus here."

"Your pronunciation is very good. Do you speak fluent Spanish?"

"Oh Yes, and praise the Lord for that. There are so many great people I would never have got to known if I didn't speak their language"

Lola looked at the parish. It was old, and with that age came the expected signs of disrepair, but there was a quaint magnificence about it. It was simple, a pinkish stucco structure with a towering spire above the front door. The door leading in was spectacular. At some point a craftsman had spent quite a bit of time fashioning the entrance, a rounded triangle above it in stained glass with the words "Most Precious Blood Catholic Church". Lola was enamored with the place for the most part. There was, however, on the southwest corner of the church, a stained-glass window that gave her pause. She thought that the window must have depicted Jesus, or an apostle, or somebody else. But when she looked at it, it only seemed to be a dark shadow.

Margaret wasn't as sure of her hiking as she once was. When she mentioned this to Lola one afternoon over lunch, Lola said she had never been to the stations before, but would be happy to help Margaret around there.

"Let's go in and pray, before we go walk the Stations of the Cross," Margaret said. Lola followed the elder lady's lead and mimicked her. She had never been to a Catholic church, or any other church for that matter. It wasn't her type of thing, but she didn't want to appear to be dismissive. When Margaret knelt to pray, so did Lola. When Margaret made the sign of the cross on her head while staring at Jesus hanging on the cross, Lola did likewise. Lola, however, did not repeat when Margaret said, "Amen", because she had no idea what that meant.

Margaret stood up after saying "Amen" and walked out the door with Lola close behind her. "I hope I am not being presumptuous," Margaret said, "but I'm guessing that if you've never been to church, you probably don't know what the stations of the cross are."

"Isn't it the story of Jesus' life told in art?"

Margaret thought about it for a little bit. "That's almost right, but more specifically, it is the story of Jesus's death told in art. At most churches, the story is told on stained glass windows. Wait until you see it here."

They walked up the path together. Lola marveled at the sheer art of the statues. Margaret stopped and prayed at each station. In between stations, Margaret told Lola what the stations meant, there were 15 in all. The first station depicted Jesus being sentenced to death, and moving on to where he starts carrying the cross, and him falling under the weight of the cross. The fourth station is where Jesus met his mother. There were tears in Margaret's eyes. "I don't know why, but the fourth station always makes me cry." Lola smiled.

They continued down, past other stations, until they came to the eleventh station, which depicts Jesus nailed to the cross. Margaret got down on her knees with nothing to protect her from the gravel against her skin. She did the same thing until she got to the fifteenth station which shows the resurrection of Jesus. "Hallelujah," Margaret said under her breath, "Hallelujah."

As they drove back down the highway to Alamosa, Margaret thanked Lola for going with her.

"I loved it," Lola said. "Thank you for explaining it to me, or I never would have understood it. The art work was exquisite though. I enjoyed it though. Sam always said that religious children have trouble distinguishing reality from fiction"

"I hope that I get to see that place again one more time before I die." There was melancholy to Margaret's voice.

"Of course, you will. I'll take you anytime you want."

"Walking that trail, takes be back to a simpler time."

"Does it make you think about your childhood and your family?

"Yes, but it so much more than that. When I was little there was only good and evil. There was only Jesus and the Devil. Now that I'm older, I realize that there is nothing that is black and white in this world, there are only varying shades of grey."

"The people of the valley, think of the people of the Plane as elitists."

"I want to change that." Margaret heard the determination in Lola's voice.

XXV

Tunnel Time

Dimitrios could hear something on the other side of the big door going into the tunnel. Other than going with Eugene, he hadn't seen much of the tunnel. It often crossed his mind to go look around, he just never walked through the door. He wasn't fearful of the noise, but nobody had knocked either.

"Fuck it" he thought to himself and pulled the door open. He wasn't expecting to see a beautiful woman with wild blonde hair, much of her petite but tight body covered by tattoos. She wore a small white dress so sheer, that Dimitrios could clearly make out her nipples. Lilith? He recognized her, but he wasn't sure of the name.

"I'm having a small party, and I was guessing that since you are new in the 'neighborhood', I thought you might want to come and have some fun. Meet some new people."

"I don't have anything to wear to a party."

"That should be the least of your worries."

Lilith grabbed Dimitrios by the hand and the started walking down the tunnel. In what seemed like an instant to Dimitrios, the two of them were walking through another door, and into a big beautiful house with the faint scent of Sulphur. Dimitrios looked perplexed at what had just happened to him. Lilith smirked, "It's called 'tunnel time'. You'll get used to it. It's pretty easy to learn. Do you want something to drink?"

"Eugene told me about Tunnel Time, but couldn't explain it to me. I'd love a double Jack n' Coke. Actually, if you don't mind, I'd like to make my own. I'm a bartender. Just show me where the bar is."

Lilith pointed the way.

"Come on," she said. "Come meet some of my friends out in the hot springs." There were naked people everywhere, men and women, all in their twenties and all attractive in some way. Dimitrios tried to take in the scene that Lilith had walked him into. There were people having sex everywhere, in the water, on beds off to the side by the stone walls, even on a flotation device. It was happening in every grouping that Dimitrios could imagine, man and woman, two women and a man, a woman and two men, a woman and woman and a man and a man.

"You know, Dimitrios, I like to throw a lot of parties. You know what would make the parties even better? A bartender, a real bartender. What do think Dimitrios? Do you want to be a bartender at my parties? The fringe benefits can't be beat."

Dimitrios smiled, and nodded affirmatively. Lilith motioned for two girls to come out of the hot springs. They walked out and immediately undressed him, and started rubbing up against him. As the two girls led Dimitrios over to a bed by the wall, Lilith told him, "Have fun tonight. We'll talk soon."

XXVI

How Do You Think the Big Fish got so Big?

Nobody ever rang the doorbell at the San Luis Valley Historical Society and Cafe, so Lee was a little surprised to hear it. He walked to the door, looked out and smiled.

"Well, hello Eugene. I was wondering why somebody would be ringing the buzzer. Hell, the door is open 24 hours a day, but it looks like your hands are full."

"Good morning, Lee. I knew I wouldn't catch you sleeping. Thought you could use a cup of good coffee and some fresh trout for dinner tonight."

"You've been fishing already today?"

"Yeah, I went to the Conejos River. I had a feeling that the brookies would be biting, and danged it I wasn't right. When the fishing is that good, it almost isn't any fun. I caught one nearly every single cast. Most of them were little guys, so I tossed them back and told them that I would be coming for them next year. But there were a few that looked like they could fill a belly up. Here. Take a look."

Lee looked inside the cooler. "My lord, if brook trout isn't one of the most beautiful fish God ever put on this Planet. The red dots on the gold scales are pure art."

Eugene handed Lee a baggie with a couple of foot long fish in it. "Go put those in the fridge, and come back and have some coffee with me."

When Lee returned, he said, "Thanks for the fish, mama will whip up some her twice baked potatoes and succotash, and we'll have a dinner made for royalty."

"I caught another one that I thought about mounting. I'm guessing he was about 21 inches, maybe four to five pounds. He put up a hell of a fight, but when it was all said and done, I put him back into one of the deep pools. He only made one mistake. I could forgive him. You don't get to be that big of a fish by making mistakes."

Lee raised his cup of coffee, to a toast. "Amen to that." The two men made small talk about fishing and hunting, the weather, and the general rumors of the valley.

"Speaking of big fish Eugene, have you seen much of Sam Coyote lately?"

"We went fishing not too long ago, but he's been pretty scarce ever since. Why do you ask?"

"A few days ago, a young man came in here. He said that his name was Dimitrios. He said he was staying at the Drive-In Inn down in Monte Vista. I've been in this here valley long enough to know what that means."

"I've had a drink with him, he was respectful enough."

"He seemed like a nice enough guy, but there was something different about him. I got the feeling that he was lost. He doesn't seem like he belongs here."

"He might have a reason. You heard about the shootings in Las Vegas right Lee? There's the wave on the Plane that he had something to do with that."

"I did hear about shootings. I can't remember how many got killed. It happens so much anymore; I get them confused. It's like they all meld together. What are you hearing?"

"Not much. Just that somehow, he showed up at Sam's house the next day, covered in dried blood."

"How'd he know to go to the Drive-In Inn?"

"Sam took him there for some reason."

Lee thought about the last thing that he said to Dimitrios, then asked if Eugene, "Is he is a Plane person?"

Eugene shrugged his shoulders. "Don't know. Nobody does. My gut tells me that Sam knows a lot more about this guy than he is letting on. Nobody can figure out what Lilith's angle is"

"Does the kid have any connections here?"

"I don't know how he could have happened upon Sam's door. You've been up there; his place isn't the easiest to find."

"Yeah," Lee took a sip of his coffee. "I guess it's not like the old days anymore, when you needed some type of connection to access the Plane. Hell, somehow that fuckin' bitch Lilith ended up here, and nobody knows why."

"Sam never said anything, but I have a feeling that she's here because of him too."

"She doesn't seem like somebody Sam Coyote would want here. Ever since Lola came around, he's tried to keep the Plane pretty quiet. He's certainly not the hell raiser he used to be."

"I tried to talk to him a little bit when we were fishing, but he didn't say much."

"This place is my home Eugene. I sure hope Sam Coyote knows what he's doing."

"That is something only time will tell."

XXVII

The Old Royal Crown Bag

Sheriff Jack called over the radio. "Matt, get your ass up to Liberty Trail. Park rangers called to say that there are three hikers who were supposed to have come home two days ago and never showed. I'm sure it's a bullshit call, but meet me up there."

When Matt the deputy arrived at the parking lot to the trail, there was a biker with a blue bandana and red scarf watching him. Jack was already out and looking around. It was close to dusk, and there was one other car in the lot. around. "See anything, Sheriff?"

"No," Jack said. "We get these calls all the time, usually idiots who don't know how to use a calendar or didn't listen to where the hikers were going, or they changed their minds about where they were going for one reason or another. Run the plates on the car"

"Should we walk up a little way?"

"I guess, at least we can say we tried. Are you sure you can make it; you look a little wired?"

"I'm fine," Matt said despite the sweat dripping off of him.

"I heard there was some new meth in town courtesy of the boys in New Mexico"

The two cops walked maybe a half mile up the trail. There was no sign of humans. No footprints on the trail, no sounds other than the breeze blowing through the pine trees. There wasn't so much as a candy wrapper on the ground. "Well," Jack said, "I'll call the park rangers and let them know that we didn't see anything. Let's go back down."

When they got back to the parking lot, Jack asked if Matt wanted to go have a beer. "I can't, Maria's making dinner. The kid's will be hungry if I don't get home."

Jack laughed, "You need to hit the glass pipe. I can't believe that you, of all people, have a Mexican wife, and are taking orders from her."

"I'm not taking orders. It's just that she won't feed the kids unless I'm there."

Jack started mocking his deputy. "Got to get home to my little spic wife and half-breed kids."

"We aren't all lucky enough to have a Nazi wife like you sheriff."

"Well fuck, I didn't say she had to be a Nazi, but you could have at least married into your own race. I wonder how dedicated you are Matt. The department had to special order long sleeve uniforms to cover up your 'white power' and swastika tattoos, but maybe it's all for show. I don't care, but some of the citizens of the valley worry about political correctness,"

"Jack, she was pretty hot before she had kids. Damn, she could suck the chrome off of a trailer hitch."

"Was that back when she was 15, meth boy?"

"Hey, she was 17 when I met her. Totally legal."

"A legal illegal," Jack shook his head. "Oh yeah, got a call from some old lady, said there was a pickup truck driving circles around the high school. That wasn't you was is it?"

"Jesus Christ sheriff, I drove past the school on the way to the grocery store, and drove past it again on the way home. I wasn't driving circles around it."

"Matt, I know where you live. You don't have to drive by the school to get to the grocery store."

The deputy was shaking and sweating and seething at his boss' comments, but he bit his tongue. Jack stared him down. "Go home to your little wetback wife," Jack said. "I'll see you at the station in the morning."

When Matt was about a mile from his house in Hooper, he pulled over in a patch of trees. He felt under the seat of the patrol car, and pulled out an old Crown Royal bag. He reached in and grabbed the glass pipe, but some meth in it, and used the small torch to fire it up. This was a routine that Matt did every night after he got off work and before he got home.

He walked into the house, the three kids all wearing only diapers, even the five-year-old. The oldest. They wanted to hug their daddy, but he walked past them and sat down at the dining room table. His wife was still in the kitchen.

"Maria, are you fucking blind. I'm sitting here and there no fucking food in front of me."

The timid woman walked down, sat the plate in front of her husband, and started to walk away. He grabbed her by the wrist, and told her to sit down. He looked her in the eye and took a bite.

"What the fuck is this shit? Are you trying to fuckin'
poison me? Fucking bitch!" He picked up the plate and
threw it at the wall. He grabbed Maria by the throat and
pushed her back in the chair. Matt took special care to punch
her above the hairline so that no marks would be visible.

The five-year-old in diapers started crying. "Shut the
fuck up," Matt screamed at him, "or you're fucking next."

XXVIII

The Treat You are in for

It was approaching midnight, and Dimitrios was sitting on the steps leading up to his room with a beer in his hand, and five more cans still in the plastic rings at his feet. He looked down at the other rooms on his level. One of them had a light on, and another he could tell had the television on. He looked at himself on the screen and back down at the other rooms. He wondered if those people could see the images being projected. For the first time, he saw a shadow in the projection house window.

It was easy for Dimitrios to get caught up in his life

being shown on the drive-in screen. Even though he was

there, and had vague memories of who he was before he got

to the valley, it all seemed brand new. When a scene came up,

he kind of recognized it. It was two in the morning and he

had just got off of his bartending shift and was taking a leak

before going to a different casino for a couple of drinks. As he

pissed, he kept thinking about the author from the

convention. He wondered about the low voice; it didn't fit the

face.

He took off his uniform shirt and was about to put on a street shirt when a voice bellowed out, "now that's what I like to see in bathroom." Dimitrios looked over and saw a man causally walking towards him. There was a sway to the way the guy walked, dancelike. He was a handsome man. Dimitrios thought this guy must have been a male model. He was tall, probably 6'5", lean physique but broad shoulders. His face appeared to be chiseled from stone, and his hair was long, dark brown with an inch-wide strand colored blonde. He stared intently at Dimitrios' chest. "You are hot"

"Whoa, dude, I'm just changing out of my uniform…."

"I'm not saying you're gay, I just said you are hot. I am gay on the other hand, so when I said you were hot, it did mean what you thought it meant. My name is Andre. And you are….?"

"Dimitrios."

"So, do you stand half naked in a public bathroom often?" Andre kept moving closer.

Dimitrios laughed. "No."

Andre kept staring at Dimitrios' body. "Can I ask you a question?"

"I guess."

"Are you gay?"

"No, I'm married, with a wife and kids."

"Awe. I see. If you're married you can't be gay?"

"Why are you asking me this? What business is it of yours?"

"It's three in the morning. You and I are alone in the bathroom of a casino, and you're half naked. Everything about it makes me horny. I was wondering if you were horny too?"

"I'm not gay."

"Dimitrios, maybe you're not gay, but I can tell you are somewhat aroused right now. You're at least curious about being with a man."

"What makes you say that?"

"If you say you were just changing uniforms, I think you would have put on your other shirt on when I walked in, but you saw the way I looked at you and you liked it, didn't you?"

"You're a good-looking guy."

"You were in uniform, huh? Do work here?"

"I'm a bartender, just got off."

"I just got off of a plane. I'm a little wound up. Did you make a lot of tips tonight?"

"It was a Monday. A little slow."

"I'll give you $500 to come to my room for an hour. I told the promoters to have the room stalked with a full bar."

"I'm not gay."

"I'll give you $750, and all you have to do is lay there and let me suck your dick for an hour."

"Nothing in the ass, right? Only you giving me head?"

"I promise."

"Let's go have a drink."

When they got to the room, Andre said, "Oh Dimitrios, you don't know the treat you are in for."

"When you said, the promoters stalked the room, what did that mean?"

"I'm speaking at the convention."

"Wow, I wouldn't have guessed that."

"You don't know who I am?"

"Just Andre."

Andre went back to sucking Dimitrios for a few minutes. "I'm Andre York. You haven't heard of me."

"Know that you mention it, it does sound familiar."

"I'm the guy that causes all of the riots when I try to speak on a college campus by people who want to censor my free speech."

"Oh, yeah, the gay Nazi dude."

"That's me. Now put your head on the pillow and relax enjoy the experience. I paid for another 25 minutes. Even after I make you cum in my mouth."

XXIX

Seismic Waves

The sun was setting over the San Juan Mountains as Sam Coyote walked into the San Luis Valley Historical Society. "I heard you missed me old man, come out and see me," he announced without having had seen Lee. There was no response. "Lee, it's me, Sam Coyote, are you around? There was not a sound to be heard. Sam walked around the first floor of the place, and there was no sign of the old man. That wasn't like Lee at all. He was usually greeting a visitor before they were five feet into the building. He had a sixth sense for what was going on around him.

Sam Coyote walked up to the second floor, and saw a small lamp turned on in the far back corner. His steps were measured as he walked towards the light, he felt hesitant. When he got back there, he saw Lee was lying on an old Victorian style sofa. His back was facing out so Sam Coyote couldn't see if his face. He wasn't sure if he was sleeping, so Sam watched the old man for a while. When finally, Lee's foot moved a little, Sam breathed a sigh of relief. He had simply caught the old man during nap time.

He turned to walk away. "Is that you Sam Coyote?"

"Yes, Lee. I'm sorry. I didn't mean to wake you. I'll come back tomorrow."

"No, Sam Coyote don't. I was just dreaming that you were coming to see me."

"Eugene told me that you had been asking about me, and I realized that it had been too long of a time."

"Look, Sam Coyote, we've known each other forever. You know who I am, and I know who you are. Between our kinds, at least in this valley it has been for the most part a mutually beneficial relationship, give or take a few troublemakers on both sides. There is something I need to talk to you about."

"Sure Lee. What's going on?"

"Tell me what is happening on the Plane?

"What do you mean?" Sam was curious about the question because he wasn't sure himself.

"Have you heard about the seismic waves being felt around the world?"

"No, haven't been paying much attention to anything lately."

"All across the world, in every ocean, thousands of miles, there are waves that indicate some kind of earthquake activity on the Planet. Scientists are baffled. There are no earthquakes."

"I kind of remember something like this happening before," Sam Coyote hung his head.

"Like I said, it always been harmonious between the valley people and the Plane people. The valley people know the psyche of the Plane. You take pity on us because of our limited existence. I know many valley people that count Plane people among their best friends. Hell, I even consider you and Lola to be family."

"The feeling is mutual for you and your family. You have always been good to us."

"The valley people are a little nervous right now."

"What are they saying?"

"Nothing that matters, hunches, gut feelings.

"Are there problems?"

"There's been a few new Plane people showing up around town. People don't know what to make of them."

"I'm sure that one of the ones you are talking about is Lilith."

"Is she the one that the bought the hot springs lodge up in Crestone?"

"Yeah, that's her."

"It sounds like she could be quite a hand full"

Sam Coyote laughed. "Yes, can be, she is strong willed to be certain, but I don't know if she means harm"

Lee raised his eyebrows. "Maybe"

"Who's the other one?"

"He's staying up at the Drive-in Inn. He said his name was Dimitrios."

"What makes you think he's on the Plane?"

"I'm not sure, but I've never known a valley person that stayed at the Drive-In Inn?"

"I didn't know what else to do with him. He showed up at my door one day."

"Do you know him from somewhere else?"

"That's the funny thing about it. I don't think that I have ever seen him before. Somehow, something told me that I needed to help the guy out. There's a familiarity about him"

"He came in not too long ago. He seemed like a nice guy. Genuine. But you could tell that behind those eyes there was something completely different going on. Controlled chaos. There's a part of him that reminds me of you, Sam Coyote, when you were younger."

"Could be Lee. It took me some time to figure things out. I'm going to let you get back to your nap."

"Sam, you know why the Seismic Wave story sounds familiar. It happened several years ago. You were still young. Although there was no earthquake activity, it turned out that baby volcano was born somewhere in the South Pacific. Nobody knew the correlation then, it wreaked havoc on the Plane world, not just a single Plane, but all of the infinite number of Planes living side by side. The force that that baby volcano injected into this fragile universe was unparalleled. It might be happening again."

"Get back to your nap Lee."

"I'll try. It's getting harder and harder to sleep these days."

XXX

Unspoken Truce

Lola sat in the bay window of a house of an old lady who lived across the street from the high school in Alamosa. The two of them kept watching out the window. "Would you like some tea while we are waiting, dear" the old woman asked.

"No, thank you. I'm fine."

The old lady looked up at her clock, "he should be coming by anytime now."

"There's a truck that just turned the corner. Is that it?"

The old lady craned her head. "No, that's too new. The one I see is old. Rusty. Different color paint. A real piece of junk."

"How many times does it circle the school?"

"Oh, I don't know. Four or five."

"Can you get a good look at the driver?"

"Oh no dear, at my age, my sight isn't too good. When he parks, I can make out a silhouette."

"He parks?"

"Usually, he parks further up, close to the corner. But one day he parked right there, at the end of the sidewalk."

"Did he get out?"

"Oh no, I've never seen him get out."

"What was he doing when he parked at the end of the sidewalk?"

"There were some girls out in the school yard. I think he was watching them. He seemed nervous; he was moving around a lot. I can only imagine what perverts do."

"That's him. It's the truck you described, "Lola said as it turned onto the street.

The old lady looked out the window. "That's it."

Lola watched as the truck turned the corner for another lap around the school. When the truck was out of sight. She ran down the sidewalk, got in her car, and waited. When the truck passed her a second time, she slowly pulled out and followed it. She was right behind as he went around school a third time before heading west. She saw the truck pull over in a Safeway parking lot. Lola spied the man getting out. He was short, and a little heavy. He had marine haircut and had a pencil thin mustache. The white sleeveless t-shirt showed off all of the tattoos. Lola knew that it was Matt the Deputy.

She got out of her car and ran up to him, "Why do you keep stalking the school?"

He was startled by her, "I don't know what you're talking about."

"I'll tell you what I'm talking about. The people who live in the neighborhood by the school are nervous for their little girls. They want to do something. They want to call the sheriff, but they can't. You know why they can't call the sheriff, because they know the driver is a sheriff. That could make the problem a whole lot worse."

"Ma'am, I am a law enforcement officer. I would think that the general public would be ecstatic that I go out of my way, even when I'm not on duty, to make sure all the kids are safe. With all of the school shootings, I make sure that it doesn't happen here. I told the sheriff he should station me at the school"

Lola looked at him in disgust. "You're a meth-mouth piece of shit. You're fucking scum. I know there is an unspoken truce between the people of the Plane and the people in the valley; very simple, live and let live. But I don't care about any of that. When I saw Victor lying there dead, I decided I don't give a fuck anymore. I don't care about sides, but I do care about little girls stalked by a drug addled pervert who beats his wife and lets his kids live in squalor."

"I don't beat my wife…."

"Shut the fuck up Matt. You know who I am. If you hurt another woman in any way. I will make your life in the valley miserable, and when I'm done with you, I'm coming after all your redneck friends"

XXXI

Chief Ouray

As Sam lay in bed, he could tell that the morning sun wasn't fully over the horizon. There was the unmistakable scent of coffee in there, but there was something else in the air. Sam was guessing that it was bacon. He could hear silverware being worked in pots and pans. Only Eugene would be cooking him breakfast this early.

Sam put on a robe, and went into the kitchen. "I could have used one more hour of sleep."

"This is an important day Sam. We need to get an early start"

"What's so important about it?"

"Ouray came to me last night"

"I thought Ouray came to you all of the time. Don't you go hunting with him."

"He shows himself sporadically."

"Has Chief Ouray told you why he still comes to the valley? He's been dead over a hundred years."

"He's my friend Sam. We like each other's company. He didn't come here this time on a social call, there's something he wants to talk to us about."

"What do you mean 'us'?"

"He wants to talk to you and me"

"Why?"

"He didn't say, but he wants Dimitrios there too."

"Dimitrios? Why?"

"I didn't ask. You don't have a conversation with the chief, you just listen"

"When?"

"Midnight tonight. There's a little valley upstream from the stone snakes, on private property. We hunt there. That's where he wants to meet."

Eugene looked out the window and saw a truck driving up the road through the trees. "Who's this," Eugene nodded out the window.

Sam got up and looked out, "that's Dimitrios." The two men watched as Dimitrios got out of the truck and dash towards the door. Eugene let him in.

"What brings you here?"

"It was a dream, I was kind of in and out of sleep, but at some point, I realized there was somebody else in the room. When I rolled over, he was sitting in the chair next to the bed. He told me that I needed to come here. Something about a meeting."

"Who told you that"

"An Indian, and he didn't need to tell me to come here. He was speaking in a language I didn't understand, but even though I didn't know the words, I somehow knew what he was saying to me. He spoke passionately, said that I needed to come here, and that you two would be waiting for me."

Sam looked at Eugene, "if it's not until midnight, why so early?"

"We'll need supplies. It's not an easy place to get to. We'll have to stay the night. It's a tough hike, nothing real harrowing, but it could probably be pretty painful trying it at night."

After the three men picked up food and gear for the evening, they started the hike up the mountain. Once they passed the stone snakes, Eugene navigated a series of trails, until they stopped at a small cabin. Eugene nodded to a trailhead, and looked up. "We have to go over that ridge, and the valley is a few hundred yards down the other side."

Eugene, despite his girth, was an excellent climber and guide, despite the frequent rest breaks. Sam Coyote had been on every trail in the valley at some time or another. Dimitrios fared better than the other two thought he would. They made it to the spot with plenty of daylight to spare. After they set up camp, and made a fire, they set up chairs around it. Sam and Dimitrios laughed when Eugene showed that them that he had done that hike with a case of Budweiser in his backpack.

At midnight, Dimitrios spotted something on the other side of the trees. "Is that another campfire?"

Eugene shined a spot light in that direction. There was a teepee there, the light of the flames was coming from inside. "That's Ouray"

When Dimitrios entered the teepee, he immediately recognized Ouray as the Indian sitting on the horse when he was leaving Las Vegas. The chief looked at him warily. He stood up when Eugene came inside. "Greetings my old friend," he hugged him before sitting back down.

Eugene introduced him to Sam Coyote and Dimitrios. Ouray simply nodded to the two men. "It has been a long time Chief. It was good that you came into my dream."

"After what I have been seeing around me, on my land, I thought that it would be time for us to smoke." He handed a pipe to Eugene who took a puff, who then handed it to Sam.

Sam looked at the Chief, "you speak English?"

"I speak many languages. In my time, it was necessary to have many tongues to keep the peace in my land. We had many friends, and many enemies." Ouray watched as Dimitrios took a puff off of the pipe. "I worried most about the enemies who pretended to be my friend. They were always the most treacherous."

"What is that you are seeing my old friend?" Eugene asked.

"There is discord in the valley that I have not seen since the white man first started coming here back in my time. We could tolerate the Spanish. Some of the early white men that were only passing through and meant no harm."

"Tell me what you mean Chief?" Sam Coyote asked.

"It comes from many directions, like the wind."

"Why did you want me here?" Dimitrios asked as the Chief stared intently at him.

"I watched and followed you here. I am not sure what to make of your soul," the Indian said. "Why did you come here?"

"I'm not sure. Some type of energy brought me here."

Ouray looked at Sam, who looked away. Then he looked at Eugene, but not a word was said between the two men.

The chief looked at Dimitrios. "I wonder what vision it is that you don't seem to be seeing. You know why you're here."

The pipe got passed around a few more times before Ouray spoke again. "I spent most of my life trying to make peace. I always thought that it was possible for all men to leave in peace. I tried to make peace between the tribes. I tried to make peace with the white men. I always believed that cooperation was possible, until I realized that some men will never want what is good for all men. They are greedy. They want power. They cannot see beyond themselves."

"Those are wise words," Eugene said.

Ouray looked at Sam Coyote. "There is a woman who walks amongst you. She is young. She recently had somebody close to her taken away."

"That is Lola. I brought her to the Plane."

Chief Ouray smiled. "She has medicine. She has wisdom beyond her years. She will carry on my legacy of the search."

XXXII

No Myths

Rarely do 911 calls in the San Luis Valley involve a crime. They are usually for heart attacks or car wrecks, and once a child got attacked at the alligator farm. Matt answered. The call had originally gone to the Alamosa Police Department, but was deemed out of their jurisdiction.

"Sheriff," the deputy said, "they found a body near Liberty Trail"

"Just one?"

"That's what they said"

"There were three hikers missing, so either there are two bodies that haven't been found yet, or there are two murder suspects on the run"

"Dispatch said that whoever found the body thought that it looked like some type of animal attack"

"Want to ride with me, or are taking the Bronco?"

"I'll drive too. Who knows what might happen?"

When they got to Liberty Trail, a small crowd had formed. A park ranger had a chain going across the gate with a "trail closed" sign. The ranger was wide-eyed and visibly shaken. "It's off the trail, about a third of a mile up. I tied a red ribbon around a tree, go west 25-30 yards."

"Have you notified anybody else yet," Jack asked.

"No, I figured that was your call"

As the two men started walking up the trail, the ranger took them aside and kept his trembling voice low, "Sheriff, deputy, if that was an animal that did it to that guy, or girl, then it was some kind of animal that I've never seen around here before. This isn't simply a body; this is a scene. A big scene. When I first saw the big chunk, it took me a while to realize it was even part of a body. What I saw will haunt me the rest of my life"

Sheriff Jack's jaw hung, despite the ranger's words, he wasn't prepared for the scene. It was a vicious sight to see.

"When I was in high school," Jack said, "I was on the golf team. We used to have early morning practice at a course in the hills outside of Denver, on one hole I hit my drive into what looked to be some kind of trash on the course. When I got to my ball, it wasn't trash at all. It was a little baby bunny, that had got caught by a hawk or an owl. You could tell that the bird had started eating rabbit's stomach first and ate its way out. There were pieces of bunny fur and blood for 15 yards in every direction. It's like the same scene to me all over again, but this time it's a human"

Matt's meth-riddled brain was not comprehending what his eyes were seeing. He was having a hard time controlling his breathing.

"Deputy," Jack raised his voice. Matt looked at him. "Call the pricks at CBI. Tell them to get down here as soon as possible. I hate the bastards, but this isn't one we are going to be able to quietly sweep away"

Matt fully snapped out of his trance. "What the fuck! What the holy fuck! What could have down this?"

"I don't have a clue. I've heard myths. But this ain't no myth." Jack looked up to the sky further up the mountain. There was a dozen or so birds circling a tight area. "There's something up there. Okay, fuck, we need to get every search and rescue team there is available. I'm guessing that we're looking for two more victims. There can't be two fugitives. There was no way this was down by two people." The sheriff took something from a prescription bottle, it calmed his obsessive-compulsive disorder. It wasn't the gore of the scene that bothered him, it was the lack of pattern, the utter chaos.

When it was all said and done, they found Carey's body two days later. Some animals had gotten to her too, but they were flesh wounds. She had been dead long before the animals ever found her. Her death scene was equally astonishing, if not only for the contrast to the scene of Dean. No, Carey's death scene was quite serene compared to Dean. She was posed on a flat rock, in a sheer negligee. The blood had been drained from here body. It wasn't an animal that did this.

Another month passed before they found Keith's body. It was a wonder he was ever found at all. His hands had been nailed to a tree in dense woods. The coroner said that he had been tortured. His dick had been cut off and shoved up his ass.

It would have been a bigger story if it happened somewhere else. The valley can be a forgotten place because a lack of cell service means no news reporters.

Margaret and Lee would get a story for the local paper.

XXXIII

The Pinched Shoulder

Dimitrios was getting used to the fact that part of his life would be playing on the drive-in screen. It was always on, whenever he looked out the window or stepped out the front door. It might have even been playing during the day time, he just couldn't see it. At first, he didn't care for the visions, but with each viewing he became fonder of it. He came to smile at the world he had left behind.

He felt an excitement seeing his bartending during the political convention. Tonight's feature on the Drive-In Inn screen was the first time that he met Wayne Bloodsworth. Mr. Bloodsworth was the president of a union of gun owners. They gave millions and millions to politicians, with the simple orders of not passing any new gun laws and trying like hell to repeal the ones that were already on the books. If you passed him on the street, you would have no idea what a man of power he truly was. He was in his late sixties with grey curly hair and a pock mocked face. He wasn't a slob, but he didn't spend too much money on his wardrobe. After he had been drinking for a while, he became hard to understand. Not so much because of the alcohol, but because of ill fitted dentures.

Wayne Bloodsworth, like most of the other speakers, found his way to Dimitrios' bar. It was the closest one to the backstage area of the speaking auditorium. Most of them made a bee line for bar once they walked out of the backstage door. It was almost one in the morning, and Wayne had been drinking whiskey and sodas since 10. For no particular reason, he took off his suit jacket, undid his shoulder holster and laid a gun on the bar. A slight panic came over Dimitrios', "Ughhh, Mr. Bloodworth can I help you?"

"I had to take that thing off, it was pinching my shoulder"

"Sir, while Nevada is a conceal and carry state, and you have committed no crime, but it is strongly encouraged by management, and especially security, that it remains concealed. If they see it, they will ask you to leave, or ask you to hand your weapon over to security"

"What kind of dumbass law is that. I said that it was pinching my shoulder, I had to take it off for while"

Dimitrios looked up to the security camera. There was a little flash. The forces would be here soon. "Nobody is taking my gun away from me," Bloodworth's tone became belligerent. There were several men with black jackets standing behind him.

"Sir, keep your hands where we can see them." They didn't draw their guns, and were trying to be as low-key as possible.

He looked over shoulder to see the security detail and Wayne Bloodsworth became irate. "You goddam motherfucker's, you ain't taking my fucking gun." As he lunged for it, Dimitrios pulled it away and the security detail tackled him. A brief scuffle drew the attention of most of the people that were gambling. "Good people of Nevada," Bloodsworth screamed at the top of his lungs. "Good people of Nevada, proud patriots from everywhere, can you see what is happening, my gun is being confiscated and I am being detained for the horrendous crime of that the holster was pinching my shoulder"

The head of the security team looked around as they were wrestling with Mr. Bloodsworth, he noticed that many of the convention goers were coming closer to them. They were forming a circle. He figured that most of the people staring at him were people likely in town for the convention. They probably had heard Wayne's speech, and they were all probably conceal and carry. He pushed the button that called the police.

In minutes, Las Vegas finest were swarming the place. A tense shouting match erupted between some Bloodsworth allies and the police. The cops were yelling for everybody to leave, or at least get back. The patrons were yelling things about conceal and carry, legal rights, the second amendment, police state, and all of the usual clichés. There was tension in the air, and it felt like a gun was going to be pulled.

It took another wave of cops to defuse the situation and

get that section of the casino evacuated. A manager came over

to Dimitrios and told him to close up the bar and go home,

they would worry about the drawer and the tips the next

night. Dimitrios grabbed his backpack and started to walkout,

but stumbled over something. He looked down; it was Wayne

Bloodworth's gun. He quickly shoved it into his bag and kept

walking.

XXXIV

Talulukang

Sam had sat down on the porch to watch the sunset.

He had seen no dust, nor had he heard a car engine. He heard

footsteps going over the gravel. He looked up, "You trying to

sneak up on me sheriff?"

"No, Sam Coyote. Just decided to walk the backway in.

Your biker friends were blocking the road. Now that the

excitement is dying down, I wanted to talk to you about the

hikers"

"What would you like to talk about Sheriff Jack?"

"Sam Coyote, as much as you like to play the simple

guy who lives on the mountain, we both know that you know

everything that happens around here. There's talk that when

you were younger, you were quite the terror."

"You give me too much credit, Jack. I don't care. I only observe. If anything, the opposite is true. There is so much going on the valley. I couldn't possibly know everything."

"Sam Coyote, what you call the valley and what I call the valley are two different things."

"I suppose. I know that you have seen things on the job, that most valley people could not comprehend, I'm sure that you have seen things you still don't understand"

"The main reason I ran for office was because I wanted to find out what the people from the Plane were all about. Neither side is supposed to talk about the other. But one of the reasons that I wanted to talk to you about the hikers, is that the valley people are feeling a little nervous right now.

"There's rumors here too, they say you are no stranger to the Plane."

"People talk. Jesus Sam Coyote, you should have seen the death scenes. Never in my wildest imagination did I think I would see a something like that. That wasn't done by anybody from the valley. Those were three kids from Littleton. It makes people wonder what is going on with the Plane"

"Sheriff Jack, there are things that happen in this valley that normal people don't understand or can't explain, so they automatically think it has something to do with the Plane, because that is the only alternative that they know of. But I'm telling you Jack, the alternatives are endless. This valley is a vacuum, there all kinds of forces that get sucked into this little speckle of a place as viewed on the face of the Earth. You're aware of my Plane, our Plane, by some fluke of the universe. But there are an infinite number of Planes of existence flowing through here"

"You know that, and I know that. I do mushrooms. You can understand why the valley people are on edge"

"So, tell me sheriff, I hear that one of the victims was eaten by animals"

"The CBI put out all the stories. They tried to give it some plausible explanation, but even they didn't buy their own bullshit. They say they're working on it, but, no they're not. There's nothing to work on. They put the remains into hundreds of sandwich bags."

"Have you ever heard of Talulukang"

"No." The sheriff was perplexed by the question.

"They legend goes back hundreds of years. A winged serpent with a forty-foot wingspan. Varying accounts of the same creature have been documented for centuries. I've heard stories about other victims. One account had it described as a pregnant Ute Indian woman who had been torn apart from the inside.

Jack looked up to the sky. "That's exactly what it looked like"

"Talulukang isn't from the Plane. There are energies that live between the Planes. They can move as they want"

"Sam, there's a group of guys. They get together all time, they've made it their mission to protect the valley, to protect their own kind. They're kind of friends of mine, they alert me when they think some Mexican is trying get into this country illegally. They're talking about forming patrols to keep track of the Plane people too. They don't like what is happening"

Sam Coyote laughed. "I know about your fucking little militia. I doubt they could tell the difference. I heard that they thought one of the bikers was illegal."

"You can laugh all you want, but those boys, those patriots, are standing up for what is right. Those hikers were all white. They're talking about retribution; they're talking about revenge"

"Talulukang didn't care if they were white or not. Sheriff Jack, you're the one that probably has the best grasp of what is happening in the valley. Don't you think it is your civic responsibility to talk those men and let them know what an unwise idea that would be? You won't win any popularity contests on the Plane. We don't bother with ballot boxes."

"I don't know if it would do any good. They're people that get pissed off when they look around them. It's not just in the San Luis Valley, it's all over the country. It's everywhere. There's a war coming. I don't know when or where, but it's coming.

"You should keep your eyes on the skies Jack."

"I could say the same to you. I'll look for a giant bird. You look for the helicopters that don't make noise. They're coming for you"

XXXV

The Throne

After a few tips from Lilith, Dimitrios was getting around by tunnel time. Once he was able to visualize it, and train his mind right, he was able to traverse the cavernous terrain of the under valley and beyond. There was so much more to it than he had expected. Some of the tunnels were so long there was no way he could still be under the valley; they must have extended into the surrounding mountain ranges as well. While exploring one morning, he went into a small tunnel offshoot. There was a door open at the end of it. Dimitrios looked in to see a man sitting on what looked like some type of throne. He could barely see the man's face.

"Dimitrios" the man called out.

The voice didn't sound familiar. "Yeah, I'm Dimitrios"

"Please come in, I've been meaning to make your acquaintance since I first heard about you being here a while back"

Dimitrios walked through the darkness until he could see the man's face. He couldn't see much of the rest of the room, but he could tell that the walls were made of carved stone. It reminded him of a medieval dungeon. "How did you know who I am?"

"Word gets around the Plane fast, actually, what I mean by that is nothing is spoken. Knowledge gets across this Plane rapidly. It's a wave. I was hoping to see you around sometime, but it was a plan that was doomed to fail, considering I like to stay on the fringe of the Plane"

"I guess I'm not on the receiving end of that knowledge, I don't know who you are"

"I guess formal introductions are in order. Sometime my brain is scattered on so many Planes at one time, I am Donovan." Donovan didn't move from where he was sitting.

Now that Dimitrios was closer, he could tell that the throne that Donovan was sitting on was on some type of alter. "Are you a King or something?"

"Here? On this Plane?" Donovan laughed. "Not quite. I think the complete opposite; I am quite likely to be the pauper of the Plane"

"Then what's with the throne?"

"It's part of the fantasy that gives me the ability to make it through another day"

"That sounds kind of sad"

"It's not. Sam Coyote and I grew up together. We were like brothers, inseparable. Something happened in our early teens. We both had separate family tragedies within a couple of months of each other. It created a schism for us for probably 25 years. We found ourselves exploring different Planes from the other guy. We both got a little wild and evil."

"So how did you end up here?"

"It's a long story that would take a lifetime to tell, but the truth is, I had spent too much time living on the high Planes. Being on the high Planes, is like being on a permanent vacation. In my case, I was living on credit, and when the bill came do, I didn't have the money. It was a dramatic fall, straight to bottom. And so sudden, like walking off of a cliff. I was looking for a dead Plane, but somehow ended up on Sam's Plane. He took pity on me, and has been generous to me since"

"So, this is Sam's Plane?"

"That's a figure of speech. This is nobody's Plane, and everybody's Plane. And that's my story. Now I get to ask you the same question you asked me, 'So, how did you end up here?"

Dimitrios thought about it for a while. "Only now, am I starting to figure it out. The day that I showed up at Sam's door, I had absolutely no recollection of how I got there. But lately, I've been having these visions..."

"Sam Coyote put you up at the Drive-In Inn, didn't he?"

"He did"

"Are the visions you see on the drive-in screen?"

"They are"

"That must be a popular place. Everybody on the Plane is doing that these days. I don't think I would want to look back on how I arrived here. I think that I would probably be terrified of what I would see"

"Like I said, I'm getting some good guesses on how I ended up here, but that's all they are, guesses"

"You should ask some of the people on the Plane why they think you're here. I know they have some pretty good ideas. Maybe go to the caretaker's house"

XXXVI

Puss Simmering Under the Surface

Sam Coyote sat down for breakfast at the UFO Watchtower Café. When Margaret brought over the menu and coffee to him, she wasn't her usual cheerful self. She had a worried look on her face, "Good morning Sam Coyote," she said lacking any kind of enthusiasm.

"It's a beautiful morning, Margaret. You don't seem like yourself. Everything okay?"

Margaret looked at him, handed him a copy of the newspaper, and finally managed a slight smile. "I've just been down a little bit lately, ever since they found the hiker's bodies. That kind of thing doesn't happen around here. Everything I've read about them is that they were good kids. It shouldn't have happened to them. It's not supposed to happen around my home. That was the hardest article I've had to write"

"I know. The sheriff came and talked to me about it the other day. He told me that the people of the valley think that Plane people had something to do with it. Margaret, I can assure you that if this was something from the Plane, I would have known about it by now"

"I know Sam Coyote. I know it wasn't you, I never meant to imply that. I'm kind of a nervous wreck, but I need to snap out of it. What can I get you for breakfast?"

"Let's do the steak and eggs. Do the steak medium rare and the eggs over easy. Margaret, dear, the Plane has its own chaos, but I'll see if anybody knows anything about the hikers"

"Will you do me a favor Sam Coyote, when you get done eating, will you go down to the museum and talk to Lee, He's a voice of reason around here"

"Of course, I will"

As Sam Coyote drove through town, he noticed that people were staring at him. He waved to the people that he knew, and they hesitantly waved back. When he walked into the museum, Lee greeted him as he usually did. About three feet in the front door, with a big smile and a firm handshake"

"To what do I owe this extraordinary surprise Sam Coyote?"

"We didn't get to talk much the other day while you were napping. I'd like to say that I came to pick you up for a nice long road trip far away from here, but Margaret asked me if I would come down and talk with you"

"That woman, God bless her. She's such worry wort"

"Well, Lee, to hear her tell it, she's not the only one. The sheriff came by my place and all but accused somebody from the Plane of killing those hikers"

Lee looked at Sam Coyote, but said nothing for a moment. "People are spooked. Strange things have been happening in this valley for hundreds of years, and they will still be happening a hundred years from now"

"Is it only what happened to the hikers that has the valley spooked?"

"From where I'm sitting, those dead people just brought the pimple to a head, but the puss has been simmering under the surface for quite some time now"

"What else is going on? I'm starting to get the feeling that I have been so wrapped up in my own little world, that I have lost touch with what is going on around me"

"Division, Sam Coyote, division. That's what the powers that be want from us. They want us to be broken down into insular little groups. Right now, you've got the bikers and the militia, they are trying to divide the valley from the Plane, even though we have coexisted for as long as I can remember with only a hiccup her and there. Back in the sixties I thought we had finally reached a point in history where we could all live in peace. Looking back on it, I don't know if it was hope, or naiveté"

"Probably a little of both Lee," Sam Coyote said. "I honestly thought that we were living in peace. I guess I need to come down off the mountain more often"

"Sam Coyote, the division is more than the Plane against the valley. It's everybody against everybody. Whites against Mexicans. Catholics against Protestants. Conservatives against Liberals. Government against the people. It makes me sick"

"Me too"

"Sam Coyote, in the valley the division is being propagated by the people who should be stopping it. That sheriff, Jack, and his deputy Matt. They don't care about upholding the law for everybody. They only uphold it for people who think like they do. They have come to view the Plane people the way that they have always viewed Mexicans"

"I was afraid of that"

"You know what I worry about Sam Coyote?"

"What?"

"Talulukang."

Sam Coyote closed his eyes.

XXXVII

Your Kind Police Themselves

Lilith opened the door to see the sheriff standing there. "Sorry", she said. "The hot springs aren't open to racist hillbillies, so why don't you get the fuck out of here?"

"If it makes you feel any better, I didn't come here to use the hot springs. I've heard stories about what happens in that water and I didn't bring any disinfectant with me"

"Okay, then. Why are you at my door you fucking piece of shit?"

"I want to ask you some questions. You can lose your attitude"

"You are taking a big chance coming here."

"Despite your veiled threats, I want to ask you questions. Of course, you don't have to answer them and I'll still go about getting the answers by any means necessary"

"If you say so," Lilith said sarcastically, "I'll humor you. Exactly what is that I can do for you Sheriff Jack? In what way can I make your job easier? Why don't you come in?

"No, thank you. I'm comfortable out here on the porch. I wanted to ask you what you know about the hikers they found up off of Liberty Trail."

"I know that they're dead, and from what I understand they met quite a gruesome death"

"Yes, they did. Did you know them?"

"No."

"Did they come here, or did you see them around town."

"No, but that's not something I would pay attention to, or care about"

"How about anybody that you know, did they mention seeing or talking to them?"

"What the fuck is this sheriff? What kind of fishing expedition are you on?"

"There are three dead people. The Colorado Bureau of Investigations is involved in this. It's all over the news. People want answers. They want to know that they are safe"

"So, let me ask you a question sheriff, of the few thousand people that live in the valley, have you questioned them all before you came knocking at my door?"

"I don't need to do that. I don't have to worry about the people in the valley. For the most part, they are all model citizens, especially the white ones. They are all God-fearing people. Even the Mexicans are in church on Sundays. The funny thing about people from the Plane, you never see them in church. I decided to start my questioning with Plane's people"

"You fucking dimwit cop. That's the type of answer I would expect from an idiot like you. So, tell me sheriff, you ever arrested any of the valley people for methamphetamine?

"Of course, I have"

"Have you ever arrested a Plane's person for meth?"

Sam glared at Lilith for a while. "No, I haven't. As a matter of fact, I've never arrested any Plane's person for anything. In fact, when I got elected, the county commissioners told me that I didn't need to arrest people from the Plane. He said that your kind policed themselves"

"Well, that we do asshole, now get the fuck out of here"

"That's not the way it's going to work anymore. I'm through tolerating elitism"

"Oh yeah, why is that?"

"I saw what happened to those hikers with my own two eyes, and I can tell you that a regular old valley person could never do anything like that. Only a monster from the Plane is capable of that kind of carnage."

"You should be hunting an animal."

"In a way, I am."

Lilith loosened the sash on her robe a bit then used her finger open the robe down to her navel. She looked Jack up and down. "You know sheriff, I never realized what a handsome man you are. Tall and lean, just I like I like them. You know why I like men tall and lean?"

"Why?"

"Because nine out of ten times, they have big, beautiful cocks. Do you have a big cock sheriff?"

"Look, I'm married…"

"Does your wife like your cock?"

"I guess, but that doesn't have anything to do with anything"

"I'm just kidding you trying to lighten the mood"

"How do you lighten the mood when there are three dead hikers, and a killer on the loose?"

"I guess I phrased that wrong. I'm telling you that you better lighten the fuck up. You come knocking on my door looking to pick a fight? You saw what happened to those hikers. What makes you think that it won't happen to you? You think that gun is going to help you? There's not a person on this Plane that wouldn't eviscerate you, you fucking idiot"

She stepped out onto the porch, and looked up at a young hawk flying. Jack turned around and started walking to the patrol car. Lilith called out behind him, "I wouldn't come back here alone if I was you"

XXXVIII

The Speaker in the Tumbleweeds

Dimitrios' had learned the nuances and perfected traveling in tunnel time. It was a simple mental trick he realized. He moved through the tunnel, at least as far as he was willing to go. Nobody had ever bothered to map out the Plane, most people said it couldn't be done.

It seemed odd to him that there was no activity underground. Lilith was gone. He couldn't tell if Sam Coyote was around or not, and there were only faint distant sounds in the tunnel.

It looked like it was going to be a beautiful sunset, so he mixed a martini and went out and sat on the steps of the Drive-In Inn. As the top part of the sphere of the sun descended below a jagged peak of the San Juan Mountains, he sensed some kind of movement in his peripheral vision. He looked over at the drive-in screen. The visions were there, but Dimitrios couldn't make out the images since there was still too much daylight.

While concentrating to make out what was on the screen, he heard a crackling sound. There was faint voice coming through the staticky noise. Dimitrios stood up to try and figure out where the sound was coming from. He looked in his room, and down the walkway to the doors of the other rooms. When he closed his eyes, he realized the noise was coming from right in front of him. The image on the screen was still too faint to see, but it became obvious that what he was hearing was coming from one of the few still standing speakers where the cars used to park.

Dimitrios walked down the stairs, and slipped into the gravel lot through a rather big hole in the chain link fencing. A squeak came from the chain of a swing on the playground due to a slight wind the sound faded in and out. It took a few tries, but he found the speaker that he wanted buried under a mountain of tumbleweeds. It was a man's voice only. It sounded like he was reading something.

When he looked up at the screen, it wasn't moving images on the screen that night, it was simply a still photo. The voice on the speaker matched the picture. Dimitrios remembered him all too well, The Reverend Cliff Black. He was the son of a famous preacher. His father was an honorable man, truly preached to people of all faiths, but his son Cliff had inherited none of his father's traits. As much as he liked to claim he was reverend, and preached what he said was the word of the Lord, Cliff Black had no interest in any of that. He was his own corporation. His ministry was run by Harvard Business graduates, weekly prayer meetings were usually followed by weekly profit meetings, no longer was it called the "collection plate", at least behind closed doors, it was referred to as "earnings".

Dimitrios didn't care about Reverend Black's beliefs, hypocritical as they may be, the reason he didn't like Cliff was because of the way he treated people when his followers weren't around. Although he never sat at the bar by the craps tables, or any other bar for that matter, it was well known to the whole staff of the hotel, what a bastard Cliff Black was.

He was verbally abusive. He once mistook one of the maids from India as a Muslim, and berated her, telling her that her religion and its followers did not belong in the United States of America. He said that Islam was a wicked and evil religion. When the maid's supervisor explained to Clint Black, that the woman was from India, he looked her straight in the eye and said, "there is nothing that an elephant with 100 arms is going to do for you honey. None of your 9000 gods is going to lead you to salvation"

The reverend was beyond rude to every single member of the hotel's staff that he came in contact with. The staff complained that he didn't even view them as humans, treating them as his own personal servants. But when he was on stage, he spoke with a soft southern accent. He could even conjure up tears when need be, like when earnings were down for two consecutive weeks.

And the cherry on top: The Reverend Cliff Black did not tip. Not anyone, for anything."

Dimitrios walked over and looked in the window of the projection house. There was an antique six-shooter sitting on a table in the middle of the room.

XXXIX

The Secret Spot

It was still dark outside. He heard the horn blast another time. Sam Coyote looked out the window and then flipped the light switch a couple of times to let Eugene know that he was on his way. He grabbed his fishing gear, a cooler, his cup of coffee and headed out the door.

In a few minutes, the two men were heading south on Highway 17. "So, where are they biting today, Eugene?"

"Ran into an old friend the other day, he gave me a map to a secret hole on Elk Creek, they don't stock it, so they're all-natural trout, and he says there are some monsters in there"

"A good fisherman never gives up his secret spots. Are you sure he isn't sending us on a wild goose chase?"

"I practically saved his life a few years back, so he owes me. Plus, I promised him that I would burn the map"

"I'll know where it's at"

"Well," Eugene laughed, "I can either blindfold you on the way in, or shoot you on the way out"

"I'll go with 'shoot me on the way out', that way I can catch some lunkers and not have to deal with all the world's colliding bullshit valley when I get back"

"I've been hearing that Sheriff Jack has been going around asking a lot of questions"

"He showed up at my place. I heard that he was at Lilith's"

"I still don't know how that guy got elected. His whole campaign was about sending Mexicans back to Mexico. The damn fool doesn't even realize that most of the Hispanics in the valley were born here. Their ancestors were setting up homes here long before the pilgrims landed at Plymouth Rock"

"He came along at exactly the right time. The whole world is moving in that direction. It's an 'us against them' mentality that is sweeping across humanity"

"I've only had the pleasure of meeting him a couple of times. He struck me as a little hostile"

"He has his own agenda, and that agenda is basically, 'whatever is best for the while protestant males," Sam said.

"I've talked to a few people who think him and his deputy are trying to start some type of confrontation between the valley and the Plane. He's even formed his own militia."

"I've been noticing the same thing"

"Do you think it's possible for him to do that, Sam?"

"It's not impossible. Whatever they're doing, they have the biker's attention, all dressed the same way. They know a confrontation is coming."

"We've lived in good will for as long as I can remember. There are valley people that I've come to think of as close friends. I can't imagine it"

"I've been thinking about it a lot the past couple of days, Eugene. I've been thinking about the hikers. I wish I could say that all it was is the sheriff picking a fight, but I'm not all that convinced that it is as simple as that, I think...."

Eugene cut him off, "Hand me that piece of yellow legal paper in the glove compartment, it's the map. I think our turn off should be coming up any time"

It took some trial and error, wrong paths and dead ends, but Sam and Eugene finally found the place that his friend had told him about. There was no exaggeration about how good the fishing was. On every cast, a trout wound up in a net. The two men engaged in a series of one-upmanship's with each other. At the end of the day, it would have been difficult to declare either man a winner or loser. They had both caught some beautiful fish that they returned back to the creek until next time.

They picked up a twelve pack of beer in the little town of La Jara, and sucked on them down during the drive home.

"Sam," Eugene was the first to break the silence, "before we got to the fishing hole, you said that you thought there was more to the tension than the sheriff and deputy picking a fight with the Plane. What were you trying to say?"

"We've both been here for a long time, doesn't anything feel a little out of place?"

"How have you been feeling? You're not quite your usual self."

"Ever since I've been here, I've always felt a strong feeling of serenity. Lately, the vibe has been a little more edgy. I've actually caught myself looking over my shoulder"

"You're sullen lately. Just like when you were younger."

"I've been thinking about when I was younger. Life was so much easier and satisfying then."

XL

The Loop

Dimitrios was fascinated by tunnel time, but it could be claustrophobic. He needed to be above ground and go for a drive. At a McDonald's for breakfast, he overheard two old guys talking about driving the "loop". He had no clue what the "loop" was, but after eavesdropping for a little while he figured it out.

The sun was cresting over the Sangre de Cristos' he pointed the truck west on Highway 160 and started driving. All he knew about the "loop" was that when you get to South Fork turn north. There was a bullet riddled sign the said "Highway 149 ahead five miles" and he figured that must be his turn. He followed the narrow little two-lane black top until he came to the old mining town of Creede. As Dimitrios drove through, he looked at the quaint little store fronts and wondered if this is what the state must have looked like in the 1800's. On the mountain was a big white spot, they called it the "snowshoe", but it looked like a face. The highway followed the river, but it was flowing in the opposite direction.

The road weaved its way through the Rio Grande National forest. Dimitrios was in awe of the beauty and the serenity that he was seeing. He stopped in Lake City long enough to have a beer and a shot. He took the final stretch of the highway until it ended at Blue Mesa reservoir. He got onto a much bigger highway there, but there was too much traffic for him, he started look for a road south.

Outside of Parlin, he saw that Highway 114 went to Sagauche and Villa Grove, from there he'd be close to Crestone. He thought about taking Highway 285 straight to Monte Vista, but there was always so many goddamn state troopers on that road. They'll pull you over for any little thing. He knew his way around the valley better coming in from Highway 17 anyway. After all, it was the Cosmic Highway.

Between Moffat and Hooper, Dimitrios looked up ahead and saw that there was a cop coming in the opposite direction. He looked down at the speedometer, he was going 71, and the speed limit was 65. "They're not going to fuck with me for six miles per hour," he thought to himself. As soon they passed each other on the highway, he looked in his rearview mirror. Sure enough, the fucking cop was doing a U-turn. Dimitrios thought about the gun under the seat, but it was fleeting and reactionary.

As soon as the cop turned his lights on, Dimitrios pulled over to the shoulder of the road. Again, he looked in the rearview mirror. He didn't recognize the cop. He had heard stories about Matt the deputy. The lawman approached the car with his hand firmly gripping his pistol.

"Do you know why I pulled you over?"

"Because I was going 71 in a 65"

"Nice try Amigo, I clocked you at 93 miles per hour in a 65 mile per hour zone. Anyone driving 25 miles per hour over the posted speed limit can be charged with reckless driving. That's a serious traffic infraction, and could count as twelve points against your driver's license"

"Deputy, I was going 71. When I saw you, I looked down. That's how fast I was going.

Matt spoke into the radio on his shoulder strap and said, "Backup"

In less than a minute, a Ford Bronco with lights on its roof pulled in behind Matt's car. Dimitrios watched as a tall, slender cop approached Matt and whispered some words to him. He figured it was the sheriff.

Jack walked over to the truck. "The deputy tells me your name is Dimitrios. Is that true?"

"How did he know my name?"

"Why are you in the San Luis Valley, Dimitrios? How long are you planning on staying?"

"I'm here for an indefinite stay"

"Oh yeah, where you staying?"

"I'm staying with a friend."

Jack stared at him for a moment. "Who are your friends?"

"Why does that matter?"

"Have you at least found some your kind?"

"My kind?"

"Dimitrios, everybody has to be loyal to something"

A rumble came from the north. "I guess I haven't found my kind yet. I'm only loyal to myself at the moment"

The sheriff looked over his shoulder as the bikers rode slowly by. "I'll tell you what, Dimitrios. Where not going to give you a ticket today. You can go, but remember, in the near future, a man who tries to be independent will perish, only you own kind can protect you"

As the sheriff and his deputy watched the truck drive off, Matt was curious. "What do you think sheriff, is he a Plane person?"

"I don't know who he is, but there is something familiar about him."

XLI

The Front Door

Nobody enters Ariel's place through the tunnel, you don't approach her that way. If you want to meet with her, you walk straight through the front door. She was never known to turn anybody away who sought her guidance. In fact, she considered it an obligation to meet with anybody in any type of need.

Ariel was one of those rare souls that sparked awe in everybody that she met. She was tall, athletic woman with slightly curly auburn hair that reached her waist. The look in her eyes was the look of confidence, she seemed to be in control at all times, despite her friendly and caring disposition. She had a savvy for being nurturing and intimidating at the same time. You wanted to hug her and get as far away as possible equally. Even in the dead of winter, her skin was always tan, her natural complexion.

To meet with her, and have a session with her, could be a life altering experience. What Ariel did for the people who sought her out cannot be defined, people need to put a label on everything, but nothing would suffice. The center itself, she likes to say, means something different to each and every person who walks through the door.

On the Plane, Ariel is the closest thing you get to a queen, although titles are considered to be low-brow. She is held in such reverence; it creates an underlying fear. That is why if you want to meet with Ariel you come through the front door. The first thing she wants to do is look you in the eyes. Sam knew the rules, that night he even knocked before entering. There wasn't even a lock on the door.

She looked out the side window and gave a big smile to Sam, and waved her fingers for him to come in. She walked over to hug him, "Sam, our waves must be connecting because I've been meaning to invite you over for dinner. Come sit with me in the kitchen, I just turned the stove on"

"That's funny Ariel, I was starting to get upset that I hadn't been invited over in a while. There are some fine places to eat around here, but there isn't anybody can cook like you"

"I love a good dinner with an old friend"

Before Sam sat down, compliments were in order. "I love the way you dress, so bohemian, so hippy, yet so sophisticated. The best part is that while you're getting dressed, you probably aren't even thinking about what you're putting on, but without any effort, it turns out perfect"

"Thank you, Sam. Would you like a glass of wine while we chat?"

"Sure"

Ariel poured him a glass. "Sam, I'm glad you came tonight. You've been in my visions quite a bit lately"

"Why is that?"

"There have been a lot of people that have come and talked to me lately. Far more than usual. I've been noticing that they are sharing one trait lately, and that's apprehension. There's tension, and it is being felt across the Plane. My understanding is that the people of the valley are feeling in a similar way. Is something going on with you?"

"People have been asking me that so much lately, I tell them that I don't know, which is the truth, I ask myself the same question over and over. I honestly don't know what is happening. On all this time on this Plane, or any other Plane, I've never experienced something like this. Maybe when I was younger."

"You have to have some ideas, Sam"

"There is something about Dimitrios. He makes me think about my life. There's a strange chemistry, like a long-lost brother"

The conversation continued onto the couch with more wine after the meal was gone. "The bottom line is that you and I have to be the magnets that hold this Plane together Ariel"

She laughed out loud as she got off of the couch. "That is the cheesiest line I've ever heard, but I love you for saying it. The truth is, we could be the magnets that tear it apart."

XLII

The Blades

Margaret tried to remember where Sam Coyote lived. She had a general idea, and it had been described to her, but she had never actually been there. Her old Studebaker ran like a charm, but she was still gentle with it driving up the winding dirt road up the mountain. The inside of her car smelled like the warm rhubarb pie that sat in the passenger seat in a basket covered with a towel.

Sam Coyote saw the slow-moving reflections of chrome through the trees. He wasn't expecting anybody, but that didn't matter because he was never expecting the people who showed up at his front door. He always kind of knew what to expect of those traveling on tunnel time to the other door, but the front door could usually be a mystery.

He relaxed a bit when he saw the unmistakable grill of the 1950 Studebaker. The drive up to his house usually required four-wheel drive. He always thought those type of cars should always be in reverse, because it looked like there was a jet engine in the front of the car. Margaret had come to see him, and he didn't mind one bit, but he was curious as to why.

Sam walked down to greet her. "What brings my favorite person all the way up here?"

"Well, Sam, when I was making deserts for the diner today, I realized that I made too many pies. I didn't want it to go to waste, and if I recollect, you were always complimenting me on my rhubarb pie, and that's what I happen to have made an extra of today. I thought that was something you might like"

"That's sweet of you. I just put on a pot of coffee. Come on in, let's have a cup, and give that pie its day in court"

As they sat there sampling pie, and sipping coffee, Margaret made nervous small talk. "Can I ask you a question?" Sam asked.

"Of course, you can Sam Coyote"

"You know I love your pie, and your company, but this is so strange. What's the real reason you came all the way up here today Margaret?"

"I'm glad you asked me that Sam, I wasn't sure how I was going to bring it up. But I like a man that wants to get to point. There's no tip-toeing around with you"

"It's a more effective way to communicate," he said.

"You're a wise man, Sam Coyote"

"So, tell me why you're here"

"I was expecting some activity last night, so I sat up on top of the watchtower and watched the skies. I was surprised that I didn't see anything. I was about to give up and go to bed. Then I heard the blades"

"The blades?"

"From the helicopters. They are quiet, but you can still hear them. The way they make them now, you can barely hear them until they are right up on you"

"I've heard about the helicopters, but never paid too much attention. I didn't figure that they had too much to do with me. Well, until the other day when the sheriff warned me about them."

"That's a position you may want to reconsider Sam"

"Why is that?"

"Do remember the other day when we talked about the tension that has been seeping into the valley?"

"Sure, I seem to have that conversation quite a bit"

"There's a lot more to it than the dead hikers, or the sheriff and his deputy"

"Like what?"

"Sam, I've heard all about the tunnels under the valley. Tell me, are they endless?"

"It depends. In some directions they go on forever"

Margaret looked down at her pie, then back up at Sam. "How far south do they go?"

"Barely anywhere at all. That seems to be some type of dead zone, but I occasionally get down to see Donovan in Ojo Caliente. I'm not sure how much further you can go"

"I don't know about a 'dead zone', but I do know that there is some type of military base under the sand dunes. That's where the helicopters ascend from, and where they descend to"

"What's the purpose of this base?"

"The government knows, and has known for a long time, that this area stretching all the way down to southern New Mexico, is the most active area for extraterrestrial activity on the Planet"

"I guess there would be a value to understanding what the universe is send our way"

"It's more than that Sam. They treat this area as a laboratory. The people and animals here are little more than lab rats. It's not just the government, the aliens do it too"

"I'm not sure I'm following you"

"Listen to me Sam, this tension has the valley wrapped up tighter than a boa constrictor. I think it's all some type of grand experiment"

"We're all ordinary lab rats"

XLIII

Culture

Dimitrios surveyed the fence around the drive-in theater. It might be cool to actually drive his truck up to a speaker and watch the movie from there. It seemed like too much work he thought. The steps outside of his room were as good of a place to watch as any.

He remembered the night that he was watching. It was a Thursday. He had the night off, thankful to be away from the madness of the convention for a while. The wife had taken the kids down to Lake Havasu in Arizona for the weekend. Dimitrios figured that was the perfect night to go out drinking. He didn't go to his casino, for the same reason that people don't eat where they shit.

Still, he ended up at the casino right next door. He knew most of the staff and they would comp him drinks, and he tipped generously in return. Usually, Dimitrios was a beer or martini man, but since he felt like getting drunk that night, he switched over to Mai-Tai's. It was going to be a painful morning, but at that point, he didn't give a fuck.

Dimitrios was trying to mind his own business, and flirt with the bartender whom he had known for years and even golfed with her husband. A disheveled older man sat down next to him, he pulled a hundred-dollar bill from his wallet and put it on the bar in front of Dimitrios. He looked over at the guy. He looked familiar. He looked back down at the bill. "Why are you giving me this? A good night on the tables?"

"I never have a good night on the tables. That's for you for the other night"

Dimitrios looked at the man again. "Now I remember, you were the guy that was drinking double Southern Comforts the other night. I still don't know what the hundred dollars is for though"

"I don't remember paying my tab, let alone tipping you"

"The gentleman you were with paid your tab"

"I don't remember who I was with," the man laughed. "Did he tip you well?"

"If I remember correctly, it was the customary fifteen percent"

The man shook his head. He picked up the hundred-dollar bill, folded it and put it in Dimitrios' shirt pocket. "Those cheap bastards. Fuck 'em"

"Thank you"

"My name is Robert, Robert Christensen." He held out his hand.

"Dimitrios." They shook hands.

"I hope I didn't get too loud and obnoxious the other night"

"Not at all, I hardly remember you. Besides, this is Las Vegas, everybody is loud and obnoxious"

"I hate coming to these conventions, and I hate speaking at them even more. The problem is that they consider me some kind of hero to their movement and they offer me obscene amounts of money to make an appearance at their little gatherings. I started a website, I speak my mind, and all of a sudden I get more attention than I ever wanted"

"So, you spoke at the convention?"

"Yeah. It was an easy hundred and fifty thousand dollars"

"A lot of the speakers showed up at my bar this week. I guess because it was so close to the auditorium"

"All the speakers they have there are a bunch of fuckin' phonies. I'm a phony. But to hell with it, were a bunch of rich fuckin' phonies. It's the American way my good man"

"It's funny, I can see the other speakers on stage, I probably even know what they are going to say. But you, you neither look the part of a speaker, nor would I have any idea what it is you might say"

"I speak about culture. Simple as that"

"What kind of culture?"

"Our culture"

"I'm still not following you"

"The culture of the white, Anglo Saxon man. We're a dying breed"

"How so?"

"Just look at birth rates. They are down for whites, not only in America, but Western Europe as well. We are slowly dying off. In a hundred years, the white man will be a shiny artifact from the past. Everything and everybody and every sex will be assimilated until we are all the same. There were will no longer be individual identity"

"So, what is your lecture about? How to stop it?"

"What I say is all bullshit. There is nothing that can be done. I give them rah-rah speeches about how if we stop the Mexicans from coming across the border, our culture can be saved. I don't believe it, but the fools who pay a $75 a ticket to hear it believe it, and that's all that matters. Capitalism at its finest"

Dimitrios took the last drink from his Mai-Tai and shook Robert Christensen's hand. "Enjoy the rest of your stay. Thanks for the tip"

XLIV

My Friends

"Help. I need help"

Lola woke up to the plea.

"Somebody, please help me"

Lola heard it again, but didn't get out of bed.

"They're dead. I need help"

Lola recognized the voice that was coming from outside her tunnel door. She finally got out of bed and went to the door. "Who's there?"

"Lola?"

"Yeah. Is that you Donovan?"

"Yes, oh thank you, thank you, thank. Please open the door"

When she opened it, Donovan was pale and dripping with sweat. He was shaking and looked like he might fall down at any moment. "Uncle Donovan, are you okay. What happened?"

He tried to speak, but dropped down to one knee. He was completely out of breath.

"Come on." Lola helped Donovan to his feet and walked him over to a chair. "Can I get you something to drink?"

Donovan got excited. "Yes. Yes, I need some vodka. Bring the bottle"

"Uncle, you know I don't drink"

"Mother Fucker, I need a drink. Or a pill. Do you have any pills, anything at all?

"No uncle, now calm down. What happened? In the tunnel you said they were all dead. Who is 'they'?"

He looked into her eyes; tears were welling up in the corner of his. He was suddenly calm. He looked away from her. "Lola………."

"What is it Donovan? I can't help you if you don't talk to me. Are you sure you're not having a bad trip now?

"Lola, some very bad shit happened tonight. Very bad. This is for real"

She loved the man, but she had a well-earned skepticism about many of the subjects that he talked about. He took too much medication, and had been doing that for way too long. "Tell me"

"Do you have a car?"

"Yeah, why?"

"I need to borrow it"

"Are you insane? You can barely standup"

"You need to drive then, Lola. We have to make sure that they are okay"

"Who?"

"Lola, will you please drive me." The tears that had been welling in his eyes were now streaming down his face.

She looked at him with sorrow. She tried to think of ways to say no, but it was fruitless. There was no way she was going to say no to Donovan. "Where do we have to go?"

"Just act like you were driving to San Luis, and I'll try to remember when I see it"

Lola kind of half-smiled and gently shook her head. "Okay then, let me get dressed"

It took a while, but once they turned onto Highway 160, Lola decided it was time to snap Donovan out the trance that he had been in since they started driving. "Donovan!" No response. "Donovan, wake up!" Still no response. She pushed his shoulder. "Donovan, you need to wake the fuck up"

It startled him. He looked around. The dawn was starting to break. "Where are we?"

"Going east on 160 towards San Luis"

He bowed his head. "Please let them be alright"

"Tell me what happened"

"I was partying with some friends in a field that had a creek running through it. The acid had just kicked in…"

"The acid?" Lola tried to stifle her anger.

"Yeah. LSD. The good stuff. Old school. Like they had in the sixties"

Lola slammed the palm of her hand onto the steering wheel. "Goddammit Uncle Donovan, if I drove all the way fucking down here and find out this was another one of your bad acid trips, I am going to be fucking pissed"

"Lola, there was this bright light. It was right above us. It seemed like you could jump up and touch it. But it was too bright, I couldn't see anything. But even without sight, I was hyperaware of everything going on around me. Somehow, the light paralyzed all of us. It picked my friends up one by one. I could hear a high-pitched buzzing, a slicing sound, and something that sounded like a vacuum. Then I could hear them drop to the ground. When I was the last one standing, I prepared for my turn. The light vanished. I looked at my friends lying in a circle around me. Then I started running, and the next thing that I knew, I was at your door"

Lola smiled at him. "We'll see.' Donovan turned and looked out the window.

After a few miles of awkward silence, with the sun starting to break, Donovan knew where he was. "In about two miles, make a right. It's about half mile down a dirt road. Stop just before you cross the creek"

After the car was parked, the two of them walked about 75 yards to a clump of trees. There in the grass were seven baby calves. Their lifeless bodies formed into a perfect circle, head to toe. Lola looked around. There was no blood anywhere. Each of the calves had had their stomachs cut open with the precision of a surgeon. She looked at Donovan. "Those were my friends," he said.

"I thought the cattle mutilations stopped a long time ago."

XLV

It's Harder to see the Clouds Coming

Donovan didn't want a ride back to town, he told Lola that there was something he needed to do with his friends. She gave a lazy attempt at arguing with him, then walked back to the car. She was still a little in shock at what she saw. The cattle mutilations had been going on for hundreds of years. There seemed to be come odd cycle to it. The valley would go several years without the report of cattle being mutilated, but when it happened again, you could be sure that there were several more to follow in the coming days.

She thought about the hikers. Maybe whatever was mutilating cows and horses had found a higher calling. Once she started thinking about the three people killed off Liberty Trail she couldn't stop. It was still early, and she was due to go by Eugene's and take the horse for a ride. Phantom rare up on his hind legs when he saw Lola. He started running around in circles in the corral. "You're worse than a puppy, Phantom"

Once saddled and bridled, Lola asked. "Are you up for a long ride today?"

Phantom nayed.

He was still a young horse, strong, with lots of stamina. He was also a smart horse. Lola knew he would be able to handle most of the trail. The funny thing about the weather, especially at elevation that high, it can change in a near instant. It had been sunny, under one of the bluest skies you have ever seen when the horse and his mount started the trek, and less than an hour in, the sky was a dark purplish color. In the mountains, it's harder to see the clouds coming.

Phantom started getting restless, something was spooking him. The wind picked up, with strong gusts. The sound it made as it blew through the pines was like thunder. Off in the distance, she heard screaming. It had started raining by then. When she looked over to the meadow, she saw a short man running. He was trying to shed off his backpack so that he could move faster. He screamed one last time as a giant shadow descended from the sky. She knew just by hearing the myth that it was Talulukang, or the Thunderbird, as the valley people called it. There was nothing she could do as the bird ripped the short man apart. It looked like a geyser of blood.

And just as fast as the weather had turned ugly, it was once again a lake blue sky. Lola looked back at the valley. There was only tall green grass. There was no blood, no screaming. Phantom started bobbing his head up and down. Lola looked up to the sky, at the peak of Mt. Blanca, Talulukang circling. It didn't seem to be threatening, but Lola turned Phantom around and went back down the hill.

She wondered if Sam was home.

XLVI

Sepia Blurs the Edges

Ariel would be stopping by later. Sam took a shower and put on his best clothes, which amounted to a pair of dress slacks, and a button up shirt. Still, it was a different from the usual shorts and hoodie. He was so confident he knew what she was thinking, he had timed it so perfectly, the door was open as she arrived.

"That was pretty impressive Sam. Kudos!"

"Let's just say I had a feeling you would be stopping by tonight"

She looked at Sam's outfit. "I don't think I've ever seen you dressed up"

"You might be right. It doesn't happen that often. I was thinking that since you cooked for me the other night, the least I could do is take you out to dinner. I've had the strong feeling there was something you want to talk to me about. I figure we can talk over dinner"

"I'll tell you what Sam, we can go out for dinner, and talk. That's fine, but we need to come back here for wine. I'm not sure it would be a good conversation for other people to accidently overhear"

"Understood"

Other nights were like being in an old black and white photograph. That's the way it was for Sam and Ariel. Sepia blurred all of the edges, everybody stayed in their own little frame. He sensed that the she was becoming irritated with all of the small talk they had to engage in over dinner.

"Let's get out of here," she said. At his place, he went into the cellar to get a wine he had been saving for a special occasion. The first glass was to get into a smooth feeling. The second glass is usually when the words start flowing.

"Sam, I've been giving it a lot of thought. It might be time for me to go and check out another Plane permanently."

The look on his face may have showed surprise, but it wasn't representative of his feelings. He wasn't even a little bit surprised. "I was wondering when you were going to start thinking about it"

"I don't feel like I gaining anything here anymore. I've been here so long, we've been her so long, it's becoming tedious"

"I can't say that I've thought about leaving. But I have been having this terrible feeling of complacency"

"It's not a bad life. I enjoyed it so much when I first got here. I loved the thrill, I loved not knowing what to expect. Now I look around and get depressed. The valley people, they just... I thought we could show them the Plane, how much better their lives could be. A few of them got it. Most of them weren't interested, or didn't have the capacity to understand it. Do you know what I think of now when I see the valley?"

"What?"

"A big fishing pier. And all of the valley people are seagulls. They wait for the fishermen to come in at the end of the day. They fight and peck until they get their share of the fish guts thrown their way by the men cleaning their catch. When they get their share of fish organs, they go home and stare at their screens until fall asleep. That's what they call that a life. I can't stand it anymore."

XLVII

The Birthday Boy

When Dimitrios opened the door, and before he could say a word, Eugene has holding a bottle of Jameson whisky in his face. Dimitrios smiled, "What's going on?" Eugene didn't respond, he held the bottle closer to Dimitrios' face, who finally gave in and took a swig from the bottle.

"You're coming to a party tonight. You don't even have to go far. It's in your front yard." Eugene pointed down to the parking lot of the drive-in theater. The place had been cleaned up. There were about a dozen cars sitting there waiting for the sun's set that was still about a half hour away. Dimitrios went to the railing for a closer look. Those weren't just cars, they were all classics, in mint condition. A '57 Corvette. A '64 Mustang. A '68 GTO. A '77 Trans Am. Not only muscle cars, there was an old VW bus, a couple of pick-up trucks parked backward so people could watch from the bed. The concession stand was even open, but because the kegs were there. Everybody was walking away with red Solo cups.

"Come on Dimitrios, put your shoes on, let's go get a beer." When they got down close to the concession stand, people that Dimitrios recognized started approaching Eugene and wishing him happy birthday.

"Happy Birthday Eugene. Is this whole party for you?"

"It's my 42nd birthday. I wanted to go all out this time around. I think the last birthday should always be the funnest"

"What do mean last birthday?" Dimitrios was a little taken aback.

"An infinite amount of time ago, when curses were all still the rage, I did something that pissed the wrong guy off. Anyway, to make a long story short, I was cursed in that I can never spend more than 42 years on a single Plane. So, at best, I got a max of 365 days left here. Probably fewer. I can vanish off to the next Plane any moment. It's bittersweet. It's been my experience that even though I'll miss this place, I get to see some slightly different version of your soul"

Dimitrios couldn't help but laugh, "That's fucking crazy man"

"I can't even remember how the curse came about, or who put it there, but the joke is on them. Their intent was to have me wandering through the netherplanes, it took me a few incarnations to learn it, but I actually learned to love it. Hey, Dimitrios go get a beer, mingle. I gotta go say hi to someone. I'll catch up with you later"

XLVIII

The Gatekeeper

Even though all the cars from the party had long since gone, there were still images on the screen. Dimitrios was tired, and wanted to get some sleep, he couldn't help but be transfixed by what he was seeing on the big white screen. Most of the scenes that Dimitrios had seen on the screen, he was fairly ambivalent too, but one haunted him.

As Dimitrios' pour a round of Mind Erasers for a group of college boys at the end of the bar, he recognized Byron James the second that he walked in. He was in his mid-sixties, he was extremely bow-legged, with a huge belly that hung over a belt buckle so big, one might think that he was wearing a boxing championship belt. He wore the same big cowboy hat, that he wore when Dimitrios has seen him on the news. The only thing that was missing was the sidearm that was usually always around his waist.

Byron James was a celebrity, if you want to call him that, around the Las Vegas area. A few years earlier, James and his son had been in a month's long standoff with agents from the federal government. At face value, the whole situation seemed pretty ridiculous. The government was claiming that he owed over a million dollars in grazing fees for his cattle on land that was adjacent to the James ranch. He, on the other hand, claimed that it was his land by ancestral rights. Basically, there were hundreds of men, separated by an imaginary line, and every single one of them was heavily armed. There were snipers on both sides lining up who their first target was going to be. And the root cause of all of this: Cows eating.

When the general public got bored of the standoff, and the news quit reporting it, some kind of agreement was reached to end it. Byron James' trial resurrected the whole issue. The only people that cared about this story was AM radio and its listeners. The trial took longer than the standoff actually lasted. James' attorneys used the 'sovereign citizen defense' successfully. Byron James was acquitted of all charges.

If James was a minor celebrity to the people of Nevada, he was demigod to the people who attended the Patriots convention. It was brilliant of the promotors to schedule him as the final speaker on the last night of the gathering. The casino was filled to capacity. Byron James himself requested that Dimitrios be the bartender for two events James was to be involved in with that night. Dimitrios' shifts would be two hours at each bar, and in exchange he would be paid a flat fee of five thousand dollars. Dimitrios was surprised that Byron even knew who he was.

The first affair was at a private dining hall on one of the top floors. As Dimitrios watched the interactions, he guessed that it was some type of party for people who made generous contributions to the "Byron James Legal Defense Fund". They were a bunch of superfans who opened their wallets wide and repeated to James what they had heard him say in his speech, then they would describe the arsenal they had back at their homes. James tried to smile and nod at them, but he couldn't hide his boredom. Dimitrios thought it was comical.

The gathering was supposed to last two hours, but James left twenty minutes early. He told Dimitrios to follow him up to his suite. The second bar was in a suite right down the hall from Byron's. It was to be an extremely private event for the speakers. Not even spouses were allowed. Dimitrios would be the only person in the room that wasn't in the inner circle.

"We got fifteen minutes before we're supposed to be there. Let's have a drink"

"What do you want?"

"What are you going to make yourself?"

"I'm a simple man, I'm having a scotch on the rocks"

"Make it two"

"Mr. James…."

"Call me Byron"

"Byron, why did you request me as a bartender? Have we met before?"

"You have a reputation. Dimitrios, I hate what the public thinks of me. They think I'm some anti-government antihero. The truth is, all I've ever wanted was to live my life on my own terms. You may not agree with most of my views, but that's fine. You're not supposed to. I'll let you live life on your own terms, all I expect is the same courtesy"

XLIX

Valentina and the Man

Her name was Valentina. She had been born in the San Luis Valley, in the home that she still lives at with her mother and six younger siblings whom she was more or less raising. Her father had been stabbed to death in prison when she was very young. Her mother started drinking after she was told of his death, and been doing so ever since. Paternity had never been established for Valentina's brothers and sisters. The best that her mom had were guesses.

Despite her environment, Valentina was smart, and for the most part intuitive. At around the time she turned fifteen, she learned that she could use her looks to get what she wanted. She was a classic Mexican beauty with long black hair and big brown eyes, her body had developed early and she looked like a woman before she was old enough to drive. A few guys thought they were her boyfriend.

All through her teens, she swore that the day she turned 21, she would get on a bus for the west coast and live the good California life. That birthday had come and went. She couldn't go anywhere, there would be nobody to care for her little brothers and sisters. Nobody had so much said happy birthday to her. She wasn't hurt, she was used to it. Even if nobody else knew or cared about the day, she would still go out and celebrate by herself.

She had heard about a little Mexican dance bar. There was enough money from waitressing in the breakfast place in Alamosa, that she went out and bought a little blue mini-dress and some new shoes. When she walked into the taberna, all of the heads turned, Valentina was statuesque.

She had been sipping a drink at the bar for an hour. A few men extended invitations to dance, but she smiled and said "maybe later." Her expectations of a celebration were slowly wearing thin.

A voice from behind her asked if the next seat was open, "Go ahead," she said paying no attention. She kept swaying in pace to the band on the stage. During a break between songs, she turned to ask the bartender for another drink, she noticed that the whoever was sitting next to her had a cufflinked shirt, and wore a diamond pinky ring. It seemed so out of place to see in a dumpy bar. She slowly looked to her left.

She could only see his profile. He was an older man, maybe sixtyish. He had dark skin, with grey hair to the middle of his back, which contrasted to his dark beard. Valentina may have grown up humble but she knew that the clothes on his sturdy body were tailor made. When he finally met her gaze, she saw his eyes were the same shade of grey as his hair.

"Hello," he said.

"Hi" She batted her lashes.

"You're cute, what's your name?"

"Valentina"

He smiled. "That's a pretty name. Can I buy you a drink?"

"Sure"

"You never said what your name is"

"I like to make people guess that" he said.

"Why?"

"It's a quick way to get to know each other. What do you think my name is?"

"You look like a 'Carlo"

"Why 'Carlo'?"

"Its like all the handsome and dashing men are named 'Carlo"

"Okay. I've never seen you in here before"

"It's my first time"

"What made you stop here?"

"I wanted to celebrate my birthday. It was a few days ago"

"How old are you?"

"21"

"Oh, fully legal. No excuses now. You are a woman"

They did a shot, and went to the dance floor. The band was playing a faster song, and most of the other customers decided to watch from the sidelines. Within a couple of minutes, the entire bar came to standstill, with the exception of the band as they watched Valentina and the man dance. It was less like dancing and more like sex with clothes on.

When they stopped dancing, Valentina begged for the gentlemen take her somewhere.

"Where do you want to go?"

"Anywhere"

"Good answer. How far you willing to go?"

"However far do you want to take me"

He grabbed her hand, "Come with me" They walked back through the kitchen area until they came to a door. "If you come with me through this door, you are going to see things you never imagined"

She looked around, "I don't get it, it's just a tunnel"

The man put a brick between the door and the frame, then gently grabbed Valentina and pressed her against the wall. He briefly kissed her on the lips, and touched her as he asked "Before you came through the door, you said you were willing to let me take you anywhere, and you will let me take you without limits. Do you still feel that way?"

"Very much"

"If I move that brick, the door will close. There is a good chance it will never open again. Now, do you still feel that way?"

"More than ever"

L

The Lady in Red

Mateo had been the star of Monte Vista's high school football team. As a running back, he had single-handedly carried the team to quarter finals of the state 1A championship. That wasn't enough to earn him a scholarship anywhere. Even Adams State down the road in Alamosa was skeptical of a player from such a small school and marginal grades. He made the mistake of deciding to take a year off of college, train hard and try to save up some tuition and walk on at a bigger school, like CSU-Pueblo.

His intentions were good, but without football there was no structure in his life. The intense training that he was committed to quickly fell by the wayside for lack of discipline. Mateo wanted it to be like it was in high school. He wanted to be an idol again. He wanted a coach to draw up the play. He wanted to be able to fuck any girl he wanted. He wanted all of the guys want to be his friend. He was barely making enough to get by at the convenience store.

As he drove across a dirt road, a shortcut out of Moffat, he thought that his job wasn't that bad. It was a great place to meet girls. He was on his way to a booty call at the house of a girl that he had met when his shift first started earlier in the night. She was supposed to be junior in high school, but had dropped out last year. She said her parents would be watching TV in the back of the house, but it was easy to sneak in her window in the front.

The short cut that Mateo was taking wasn't quite the way he remembered it. He was supposed to driving south, but the compass on the dashboard of his car said he was going due west. The dirt from the road was fine, and slowly covering his headlights making it difficult to see. There was some type of reflection up head. He was hoping it was some type of road sign, but from a distance it looked red or pink.

As he got closer, he saw that the reflection was coming from something in the center of the road. Mateo slowed down and as he approached; he could see that it was a person. It was a woman. She didn't budge as the car slowly came to a halt. Once he stopped, the woman started walking to the passenger side of the car. She wore only a strapless red dress. Mateo wondered how she could walk in such high heels in the dirt, but she made it look effortless. He rolled down the window, and she leaned inside. "Have you been thinking that you were lost?"

"The road isn't like I remembered it. I must have missed a turn"

"Compasses can get funky around here, I've seen them completely spin. It's crazy, but don't worry, I'm here to show you the way"

"Get in, tell me where to go"

"No, turn off the car. We have to walk from here. Look ahead, there is no more road"

Mateo didn't think too much about what was happening, he knew that he wanted to fuck the lady in red. She came to what looked like a piece of plywood in the middle of a field. She turned around and studied him. "Do you want me to fuck you like you've never been fucked before?"

"Oh, yes"

She pointed to the plywood. "Lift the left side of that"

"What's a stone staircase doing in the middle of a prairie?"

"If you go down those steps, I'll show you a world beyond your imagination. It's endless down there. You may never be able to find your way back"

Without hesitation, Mateo walked down the stairs.

LI

The Thread

Dimitrios cursed under his breath at what he saw on the screen. He knew these visions would eventually come. He thought about putting foil in the window and sealing off the front door, but he knew that they would be over soon.

As he watched, he was having a drink with Byron in the suite, he still wondered why he took the gun to work that day. He started thinking about it after he hung up from his wife. She told him that she wasn't coming back from Lake Havasu, and neither were the kids. She told him that she didn't know him anymore. He said he understood and hung up.

That day had been dreamlike for Dimitrios. He wondered if he was dead, and the stories of your soul watching your body were true. He wasn't completely out of his body, but he wasn't all the way in it either.

When he first walked through doors for work around four in the afternoon, he saw Richie, the internet troll, running up to him, "I heard you're going to be the private bartender at the speakers party tonight"

"Yeah, so"

"You have got to get me in there"

"No"

"Those are my heroes"

"Are you fucking kidding me?" Dimitrios shook his head.

"I have $2500 I can give you"

"What? Those people are con artists. They don't care. They'll say what anybody pays them to say. Anyway, I thought you put this conference together."

"I lied. You don't understand Dimitrios. Those people are the last true Patriots. They are the thread holding this country together. They are inspiring. They're teaching us to rise up and make this country what it once was"

"Look, fuck all that. This party is on the top floor suites. There is no way to sneak you in. The security up there is intense. They have ex-military guys from all over the world up there. They are some bad mother fuckers"

"Okay" said Richie politely. He walked away. Dimitrios watched him until he was out of sight.

The incident had slipped his mind as he poured a drink for Andre York, who was asking what Dimitrios doing after work. Before he could answer, there was a loud crash. Richie came crashing through the door. He was covered in blood, that may have been his own and he had a gun in his hand. He staggered towards the bar. Without hesitation, Dimitrios pulled out the gun he had hidden during the Wayne Bloodsworth confrontation, and aimed it at Richie's chest. When pulled the trigger it blew a hole in Richie's heart. Dimitrios went over and stood over the quivering body. The blood seemed to coagulate on the carpet quickly.

LIII

Make Me Like You Are

"What is that you like about women?" The lady with strapless red dress asked Mateo.

"Everything, I like everything about them"

"Like what?"

"I love their asses. When I see a nice ass it's like I get in a trance. I like their tits too. But they have to be the right size, not too big, and not too small. Oh, and natural tits. I don't like that fake silicon bullshit. I want the real thing"

"So, you like tits and ass. That's quite a revelation. Anything else you like about women?" Lilith shook her head.

Mateo had to think about it. "It's always nice when they have a pretty face"

"You could just put their face in a pillow"

"I guess"

The lady in red smiled. "I think I have this. You like nice asses, perfect sized tits, and a pretty face. You are quite the renaissance man, Mateo"

"Even it they don't have a pretty face, as long as they have a nice ass, I can do them from behind"

She bit her lip. "What about talking to them? And listening to them?"

"Oh yeah, I listen"

The lady in red walked over to Mateo and started rubbing his chest. "I want you to listen to me," she moved her hand down and started rubbing his crotch. "Will you listen to me? Will you do everything I tell you to do?"

"Anything you want"

She grabbed him by the hand, and led him into a room that was completely done in white tile, the walls, the ceiling, even the drain in the middle of the floor was white. Suspended from the ceiling was a bar about three feet long. There was a single handcuff bracelet at each end of the bar. She made him take his shirt off, then the lady in red put Mateo's wrists into the cuffs. She walked back and looked at him. "How does that feel?"

"Damn, lady, this is some kinky fucking shit"

She turned around so that her back was to him. She bent over and grabbed her ankles, held it for a few seconds, then slowly went back up and extended her arms in the air, then lowered her right arm down to them hem of her dress. She pulled them up to her waist, "What do you think Mateo, do I have a nice ass?"

"Oh yes, it fucking perfect"

The woman walked over to the hanging young man. "You know what I like, a big fucking dick. Do you have one of those?" She undid his belt and pulled his pants down. She got down on her knees before she pulled his underwear down. She rubbed the bulge under the material. "It has promise." In a quick move, she pulled his underwear down. His erect cock was in her face. She kissed it gently on the head, and then stood back up. "That's a nice dick, Mateo"

"I can't wait to put it inside you"

"In time"

The lady took off her red dress. She was naked in front of him. "How about my tits, are my tits the right size?"

"Oh yeah, they're fucking perfect. Are you kidding me?"

"I'll bet you would say that to any naked girl standing in front of you"

"No...."

"Let's see." She went over and pushed a button in the corner of the room. The wall opposite of the door started rising up, another white tile room was twice its size. In the middle of the other side of the room was a girl also handcuffed to a bar. Mateo saw that there was a nicely dressed, grey haired man sitting in a lounge chair.

"What do you think, does Valentina have nice ass and perfect tits?" The man asked.

A wave of fear overcame Mateo. He could tell that the Valentina had been crying. "She does," he said softly.

The lady went over to where the older man was, and sat in his lap. She alternated looking at the two handcuffed souls. "They are a couple of nice-looking kids. Maybe we should let them fuck each other first. It could be fun to watch"

The man stood up. As he walked over to where Mateo was hanging, he was taking off his cufflinks and unbuttoning his shirt. He stood in front of the young man and stripped to his waist. Despite his age, the old man was a mountain of muscle, with seemingly every vein in his body visible under his skin. "They are a good-looking couple," he said. He walked over to where Valentina was hanging. Gently, he pinched her nipples and kissed her on the cheek. He undid his belt and let his dress slacks fall to the floor. He spread Valentina's legs apart and rubbed the head of his dick rub against her clit. She shuddered.

Walking back to where the lady in red was standing. He lifted her up by the throat and slammed her against the wall and thrust his dick into her. He pounded her mercilessly. She started grunting, that slowly turned into a growling sound. Mateo started hyperventilating as he watched the lady's leg transform from a human into that of animals with a hoof. Dark black, coarse hair grew out of the follicles. Her face stretched forward until she had a snout and her mouth had fangs. The harder the grey-haired man fucked her, the redder her eyes got. After one last violent thrust, he threw her to the floor.

On all fours, she ran over to Mateo and lunged at him. She sank her fangs into his throat and started gnawing. His body convulsed. As she is locked into his throat, her cloven feet were constantly flailing, the hooves cutting deep gashes into his legs. There was too much blood for the drain to handle. Eventually, his body went limp. The lady released her jaws from his neck. She started her using her fangs to bite and tear away the area around his genitals until she chewed his penis off, still intact. She took it into her teeth and over to where Valentina was hanging and dropped it on the floor.

The man walked over and picked it up. He looked over to the lady who was slowly transforming from animal back into human form. When she was fully changed back, he showed her the penis. "Maybe we can watch them have sex after all," he laughed.

"Put it in me," Valentina said.

The man and the lady looked at her suspiciously. "Come again," he said.

"If you put in me, will it make me like you are?"

He started rubbing the penis around her lips. "You sure you want to be like us?"

"Yes"

"You're not afraid to die?"

"I've been dead for a long time," Valentina said. "Now, I want to be alive"

The old man threw the penis over to where Mateo's body was still draining out. He held up his hands. Valentina watched as his fingertips transformed into claws with razor sharp points. He dragged them across her throat and chest. They created little cuts that left tiny little droplets of blood. The lady in red licked the vital fluid away.

With force, he slammed the claws into Valentina's ass, puncturing and tearing deeply. Simultaneously he rammed his dick up inside or her. His breath was like fire on her neck as he violently fucked her. He looked in her the eyes and she watched until there were flames in his pupils. Gold horns started growing out of his forehead. Every thrust inside of her came with more fury. The last thing she remembered before passing out was the sight of her blood going the down the drain.

When Valentina woke up in the morning, she was in a big bed. She felt especially serene and relaxed. She didn't recognize her surroundings, but she felt as though she was being watched. She looked to her right, there was a woman smiling at her. To her left was a man, he was smiling as well. The woman spoke first. "Good morning Valentina. You probably don't remember us, but I'm Lilith and that is Dimitrios. Welcome to the Plane. You are going to fit in nicely here"

LIII

An Ominous Song

Lola kept driving to all of the parking lots at the Great Sand Dunes National Monument. At the northern end of the park, she finally saw Lee's old Chevy Blazer. She looked on the map for the Upper Sand Creek trail. As she walked, she saw a broken piece of mirror on the stand. She looked at it, and noticed that the jagged edge was pointing west. It looked like there had been footsteps going that direction, but it was hard to tell with the ever-shifting sands. She picked up the mirror and followed the steps.

As she came over a hill, she saw Lee sitting in a lawn chair. There was a picnic basket at his feet, and empty lawn chair next to his. Lola sat down. "That's perfect timing, it should begin anytime now" He pointed to a black cloud rolling down off of the mountains. "When that is overhead, I'm sure that will be when we hear it"

With the approaching cloud came a low, deep hum from the ground. The closer the cloud got, the greater the vibration of the hum got. As if on some great cue, other frequencies of humming were becoming audible, some higher, some lower. A wind followed the cloud, it turned the humming into a cosmic orchestra.

"It is a haunting song that the sand is playing," Lola said.

"I find it a little melancholy. It sounds like weeping over sounds of joy. It is the sound of loss. Beautiful, but sad"

"Eugene used to bring Sam here when he was a boy. We must be hearing something completely different. What I hear is the music that they play before a shark eats somebody in "Jaws".

As the cloud moved east, it took the song with it. As they sat there in the emerging sun. "How do you know when the sands are going to sing Lee?"

"I was born in this valley, a long, long time ago. This place has a rhythm to it. It's there for everybody to hear, but most people, valley and Plane folk alike, are too wrapped up in themselves to listen. If you listen to the rhythm of the valley, you'll learn when the sand will sing"

"Are the songs always that ominous?"

"It's usually a little higher pitched, there's an airiness to it. The clouds aren't usually that black though"

LIV

Roll up your Shirt Sleeve

It was windy on the walkway of the Drive-In Inn, and Dimitrios could hear thunder coming from the west. A half dozen dust devils danced around the parking lot, driving the tumble weeds to the outer fences. Above it all, the screen continued its movie.

There he was, standing over Richie's body. Congressman Longstreet ran over to Dimitrios and slapped him in the in the back. "That was beautiful my son. Fuck all of those ignorant little peons screaming for gun control. This is living proof, that every man, woman and child in this country should be armed. A man who defied authority with his gun, has become a hero for the ages." Wayne Bloodsworth from the gun lobby stood up and started clapping. "Finally, the good guy," the congressman continued, "had a gun to counter the bad guy's gun. You're coming out on the campaign trail with me"

Dimitrios raised the gun from his side and put the tip of the barrel to the politician's forehead. "Go sit down," he ordered Longstreet. He pointed the gun at Bloodsworth, "you too". He scanned the room. "All of you, sit down." The congressman was still stumbling around when Dimitrios grabbed him by the back of collar and dragged him into a chair by the bar.

Dimitrios put the barrel of the gun Congressman Longstreet's temple. "Look at that kid", he nodded to Richie's body. "That kid looked up to you. He made you. He bought into all of your bullshit. He bought into your fear". Dimitrios looked around the room, "he bought into all of your fear. Just this morning, in the lobby of this casino and he told me that he thought you were Patriots. I told him that you were all thieving dogs that only had one master, the dollar bill. He wasn't breaking in here to harm you, he ended up dying here because he idolized all of you idiots"

Dimitrios looked out of the room's door into the hallway. There was no activity, not a sound. Whatever Richie did to casino's security system to get in, he did it well, hacked the system. The top five floors of the building were completely sealed off from the rest of the building, and each of those floors was individually sealed. Nobody would be up her for at least an hour. Dimitrios remembered that fact from his new employee security training.

He walked back and stood in front of the congressman who was visibly shaken. "Roll up your shirt sleeve" Longstreet did as he was told. Dimitrios put his arm against it. "Look at that" Dimitrios laughed, "almost the same color. All this time, you've been worried about the blacks, and the Mexicans, and the gays and people you don't want using a certain bathroom. How fucking ironic, that at the end of the day, it was a straight, white male that got you"

Dimitrios shot Congress Longstreet in the eye.

LV

Old Scratch

Sam Coyote was in the corner booth of the UFO Café, reading the Alamosa Valley Courier. There wasn't a whole lot of news in there; most of it was puff pieces designed to do nothing other than fill column inches. There's a blurb about you if you are issued a summons for running a red light. If it's a slow news day, you might even find out that one of your neighbor's cats died.

As he read, a somber voice asked, "Mind if I join you?"

Sam looked up to see Lee standing above him. "Of course, you can, in fact I've been meaning to buy you breakfast for a long time"

"That's mighty nice of you Sam, but you don't have to do that"

"Nonsense, I insist."

"Well, thank you good sir"

Sam Coyote studied Lee as he sat down. His movements were measured and he looked a little pale. The smile that Sam thought never left Lee's face was gone. The old man was wearing an aura of defeat.

"What's the matter Lee? You're not looking so hot"

"Oh, I'm alright Sam. I haven't been sleeping too well, and my appetite hasn't been too good. I think its kind of hurting mama's feelings"

"Have you been to the doctor?"

"I don't think that there is anything that a doctor can do. They wouldn't have the training for that"

"What's going on?"

"Chaos, Sam. Chaos"

"I don't understand"

"There's two local kids missing, nothing is official, and most of the public doesn't know"

"Maybe they ran off together"

"That's the thing, they haven't been heard of since the same night, three days now, but there is nothing to suggest they even knew each other"

"Who are they?"

"One of them you probably know, his name is Manteo. He worked his shift at the convenience store at the end of town, went to see a friend. They found his car in a field north of Hooper. There was nothing in it to give clues about where he might be"

"I do remember him. He was a hell of a running back. Who else?"

"Her name is Valentina. Nobody knows too much about her. She grew up south of town a way. Supposedly, her mom is a drunk and druggie, and Valentina cares for her baby brothers and sisters. She just turned 21. One thing that everybody can agree on, she's quite the looker, very beautiful"

"A beautiful 21-year-old girl? She probably realized that there's a great big world outside of the San Luis Valley, and took off"

"According to her mom and a neighbor, there's no way she would leave those kids"

"Is Sheriff Jack investigating?"

"Yeah, I talked to Jack"

"Are the kids Mexican?"

"Yeah"

"I wouldn't be expecting the sheriff and his deputy to work too hard on finding them"

"I don't know about that Sam"

"Why? You know who and what he is"

"Sam, I'm not sure how to tell you this"

"What? You know me, just say what's on your mind Lee"

The old man looked at his companion with weary eyes, and then down at his coffee. Sam could tell that he was nervous. "Tell me what it is you need to tell me Lee"

"Valentina was last seen at a nightclub in Monte Vista. While she was there, she was dancing rather provocatively with an older gentleman"

"So, trust me, there are a lot of girls out there that age with some type of daddy issue"

"The older gentleman was impeccably dressed. He wore a black collared shirt with cuff links. They walked into a room behind the kitchen. They never came out, and neither has been seen since"

Sam sat his coffee down and stared out the window. He started pounding the side of his fist lightly on the table. "Are you sure about this?"

"Every witness tells a version of the same story"

"Old Scratch"

"That's what I was thinking too Sam. Now you know why I haven't been sleeping well or eating too much"

Sam nodded in agreement. "What did the sheriff say when you talked to him?"

"Nothing really. He didn't seem too interested"

"Fuck! I thought that bullshit was gone forever"

"Sam, you might be right that Jack won't work the case too hard because the kids are Mexicans. On the other hand, if he finds out that has anything to do with the Plane, he is going to make life difficult"

"That's what I'm afraid of"

"Sheriff Jack might be a lot of things, but stupid isn't one of them"

LVI

The Middle of the Road

Ariel spent most of her time in a meditation room on the top floor of her spiritual center. She designed it to be all glass, so that she could see the entire valley. She believed that the sun was vital to the growth of the soul. She didn't like the that the place was connected by tunnel, she had never seen that on any of the Planes that she had been on before. While meditating, a horrible vision came to her. She opened her eyes at exactly the same time that she first heard the sound.

There was a reckless car driving through the town, coming her direction. She was furious that somebody would be driving like that in a peaceful place. She got up and walked down the stairs, straight out the front door and into the middle of the street. She couldn't see the car yet, but she knew it would be coming over the hill any second. When she saw the windshield of the car, it started skidding, and with the loose gravel, it was fishtailing. Ariel didn't move an inch from spot, nor did she even flinch.

After the car finally came to a stop without miraculously hitting anything, Sam got out of the driver's side door. He was out of breath and visibly shaking. "What in the fuck are you doing standing in the middle of the motherfucking road? Are you fucking stupid?" He was so pissed off that he was spitting as he was talking.

Ariel glared at Sam. She made eye contact with him, and didn't lose it as she slowly walked toward him, and it was still there when her nose was within a couple of inches of his. Her words were calm and measured. "What in the fuck are doing driving through the motherfucking town like that? Are you fucking stupid?"

Sam took a few deep breaths and composed himself. "I'm sorry. I am, but I think that we need to talk"

"About what?"

"About something that shouldn't be discussed in the middle of the motherfucking road"

"I was meditating. A lot of people do that around this time of day"

"Hey, I said I was sorry"

"And it was so sincere." Her sarcasm was thick.

When they got up to the room, Ariel poured the two of them some tea and they went and sat on the floor. "So, what's so important that it's worth wrecking the environment for?"

"I ran into Lee at breakfast a while ago. Did you know that there are two kids from the valley that are 'missing?"

"I heard something in passing, but I figured a couple of lovers ran off together"

"That's what I thought too. Except they didn't know each other. Anyway, I wasn't concerned either until he told me about the girl"

"What about her?"

"She was last seen with an older guy. He was nicely dressed, wearing a bow tie and a shirt with cufflinks"

Ariel closed her eyes and bowed her head. She stayed like that for a minute then put her tea on the floor and stood up. "The people in the valley used to believe that seeing Old Scratch himself was a Hispanic myth and it was easily dismissed. People are more sophisticated now. They know about the Plane. There's always been a hint of tension between the two. Lately, I've sensed that the tension is growing, I can feel it when I walk on the ground. If this turns out the way think it will, the tension will turn into hostility. They will know it's not a myth, they will know it's the Plane"

"I know"

"Sam, you know that I have to ask you?"

He nodded in agreement. "Ask"

"Was it you?"

"No"

"You've done it before"

"I know. I was young. I'm not making excuses. What happened is what happened. I can't change it. I liked going on to the dark Plane, at the time it was fun, but those days grew to bore me. I guess that's what happens with age"

She looked at him and shrugged. "What about the boy?"

"Nobody knows. I think they found his car in a field across the highway from here"

From the window of her meditation room, Ariel was watching as a young girl with long dark hair walked out of the hot springs resort across the street.

"Nobody huh. I'll bet a lady in red saw it all"

LVII

The Joke

The same night played on. As he watched, Dimitrios wondered why there were no good scenes of his previous life showing. Where were the home movies of him with his wife and kids, in the early days, when times were good? Why was it all that same week in Las Vegas playing out over and over again?

Congressman Longstreet's body was at a ninety-degree angle to Richie's. Dimitrios noticed for moment that the two of them appeared to have different colors of blood, varying shades of reddish purple. Richie does look more serene in death than the congressman did. Of course, looks can be deceiving.

Dimitrios looked over the people in the room. He deliberately tried to make eye contact with any of them. "You people talk so tough when you're up there giving a speech," he said to nobody in particular. "Here I am, the bad guy with the gun. One of you patriot heroes has to have smuggled a gun past security. One of you true Americans has to have a piece. Everybody in the country has heard your talk. Now it's time for action. Now it's time for you to take me out and you can be the same savior that you see in your own head"

"Please," Eleanor Prudhome cried. "Put the gun down. You can still do the right thing. This isn't funny anymore"

Dimitrios aimed the gun at her, and pulled the hammer back. "This isn't funny? You don't think this is funny?" He walked over and put the gun to her mouth. "Answer me you fucking bitch! I'll ask you again. 'Don't you think this is funny?"

"No," she whispered through tears. "No, I don't"

"You see, Eleanor, I seem to recall you saying that this was all a joke. And it was joke that wasn't meant to end in laughter. It was a joke that was supposed to end with anger. It was a joke that was supposed to end with more division. Don't you remember telling me that Ms. Prudhome?"

"I'm an entertainer, a performance artist, this is my job. This is what the public wants from me"

Dimitrios laughed. "Geez, Eleanor, I guess I misunderstood you as a person. The way the joke is supposed to end for you is with a big fat bank account. The joke isn't even about laughter or anger, it's about the dollar"

"It's how I make my living"

"Stand the fuck up" Eleanor didn't move. "You better stand up right fucking now or I'm going to paint the wall behind you with brain tissue and bone fragments"

She stood up. "Lean your head back," Dimitrios told her. He walked over and inspected her throat. "Were you born a woman Eleanor?"

"No"

"I've always wondered about the Adam's apple and the deep voice. I could never reconcile it in my mind. Here was somebody saying vicious things about homosexuals and transgender people, but you were obviously a man at some point. It made no sense to me"

"Like I said, it's how I support myself"

"You sold yourself out for a buck. I hope it was worth it" The hammer of the gun hit the back of the bullet.

LVIII

Insular Immunity

For whatever reason, Lola had never been to the spiritual center. Ariel had never been anything less to her than friendly, charming and polite. Still, there was something about the place, and Ariel herself, that intimidated her. She had grown up hearing Sam singing the praises of Ariel and knew that she would be welcomed into the center, but it never happened. Lola often asked herself what it was about the place that made her apprehensive, but all that she ever came up with is that she didn't feel spiritual even a little bit. How could a nonspiritual person expected to be welcomed into a spiritual place? she thought to herself.

Lola didn't feel any trepidation as Ariel ended up standing next to her at an art gallery in Salida. It was the opening night of an exhibit by a teenage girl who lived down the street from the spiritual center in Crestone. "I never would have expected this kind of theme in art from her," Ariel said to Lola. "When she comes into the center, she would seem to be a fount of positivity. I would have expected the colors of her paintings to be bold and bright"

"I don't know her personally, but this certainly does not match the type of art I envisioned in my head from a teenage girl. These pieces are all so dark. It just surprises me"

Ariel looked at her quizzically. "How come you never come to the spiritual center?"

"I guess that I've never considered myself to be a spiritual person"

"That doesn't matter"

Lola let a tinge of guilt get to her and went to the spiritual center. Ariel was there to greet her at the front door. "Welcome Lola, I still can't believe you've never been here"

"I've always wanted to"

As Ariel showed her around the place, she asked, "So tell me Lola, why is it that you've never considered yourself a spiritual person?"

"I don't know. Sounds like a waste of time. It doesn't strike me as something that is real. Making excuses for a shitty world"

"I hadn't thought about it that way. Why do you think the Plane is such a shitty place?"

"I'm not speaking specifically about this Plane. I'm thinking about the big picture. All of the Planes together. It's just kind of fucked up. I need to find a way to change it. I owe that to Victor"

As they walked into the meditation room, with glass walls that overlooked the valley, Ariel said, "I guess I'm kind of immune to all of the ugliness. I tell myself that I have seen worse"

"How can you not be?" Lola did a half circle pointing with her finger to the amazing landscape below. "It's hard to see reality from way up here. If I looked out these windows every day, I would think the Plane was perfect too"

Lola could tell that Ariel was not happy to hear that. "Oh, I am so sorry Ariel, that kind of came out wrong"

"Actually, Lola I don't think it did it all. You might be right. Maybe I have become too insular up here. I used to care about this Plane very much. When I first got here, I thought this was the perfect place. After being on so many Planes over the course of time, I figured this would be the one I would spend infinity on"

"I think you can physically be on the Plane, but not be there at all"

"For somebody who isn't spiritual, that's a spiritually profound statement to say"

"I've talked to Sam about it quite a bit lately. He says he feels the growing acrimony of this place, and he has alluded that you may be thinking the same thing, although I don't know that for sure"

"Sam and I have discussed the dynamics of the Plane and the valley and everything else"

"He's told me. I've heard his take on the growing hostility. I love him, but I'm not sure he has real grasp of what is happening. The laws of the valley are being are being enforced by the lawless, and although there are no laws of the Plane per se, just understandings, I'm getting the feeling that people are coming here for that reason. Not the reason that you and I are here"

"Lola, you may call yourself nonspiritual all you want, but the truth is you may be the Dalai Lama of the Plane"

LIX

I Matter

Dimitrios found himself laughing as he watched the old him on the drive-in screen shoot Eleanor Prudhome in the back of the head. He laughed even harder when he saw Andre York scream and cry as her body hit the floor in a crumbled mess.

"What the fuck are you crying about bitch? You aren't the one who is dead. Yet"

"Please don't kill me"

"What makes you think I'm going to kill you"

"Because you just killed three other people" Reverend Cliff Black yelled from the couch.

Dimitrios scanned the room with his gun randomly pointing at the others. "Is that what all of you think? That I'm going to kill all of you?" He looked around the room. The remaining of the convention speakers were all nodding yes. "No, no, no, I'm not going to kill all of you. There's going to be two of you that are going to walk out of here alive. You will be traumatized and scarred for the rest of your life, but you will be alive, and you will be better for it, because you will have made it through one of your deepest fears"

Dimitrios walked over to Andre. "Why did you scream when I shot whatever her name was?"

"It's a horrible thing to see"

"How do I know that you weren't acting. That's pretty much what you are, right? An actor"

"I'm a respected political commentator"

"You're a fucking joke. You are afraid to be alone, because that means you're not getting any attention. That's why you'll pay a $1000 to some random guy in a bathroom to give head to, because you're too fucking afraid to be alone, am I right?"

"You know you are"

"I doubt that you even plan what you're going say when you walk out on stage, you pay attention to the crowd, then say the most outlandish thing that you can think of, because all you want is attention. That's a despicable way to go through life"

Andre York stopped whimpering and got angry. "Despicable life? Is that what you said to me? You know what bothers you the most about me?"

"Please, do tell" Dimitrios aimed the gun at Andre's forehead.

Andre took a step closer to the gun. "I fucking matter. That's what bothers you. There are riots on college campuses because they want to violate my right to free speech. You are a bartender, the only time you remotely matter in this world is when somebody needs a rum and coke. The whole reason we are in the room together is because We all matter, and you don't. You're a lowly bartending piece of shit. If you couldn't pour an appletini, you'd be watering my garden"

"Give me a name"

"Pardon me?"

"Give me the name of somebody that you truly matter to"

"Do you know how many followers I have?"

"Just give me one fucking name"

Andre York looked to the other people in the other room. He fumbled for words"

"You don't even know their name's, do you?"
Dimitrios asked. "You probably heard them a hundred times
this week, but you're so wrapped up in yourself, you're
oblivious to anything that isn't getting you attention"

"I matter"

"No, you don't" Dimitrios put the gun to Andre's lips.
"Since you like things in your mouth"

LX

Blood for the Sake of Blood

By word of mouth, everybody knew that that there were two kids were missing. When the sheriff confirmed it to the Alamosa Valley Courier, a quiet fear descended on the valley. The wounds of the three hikers had not even yet begun to heal, but this was different. The hikers were all from Denver, they were faceless. Valentina and Mateo were valley people. Both of them had been born and raised in the same place that they went missing.

Sam Coyote had seen the front page of the newspaper. He thought about Margaret and Lee. What was he going to say to them? He had known them for as long as he had been on the Plane. There was no way he would be able to lie to them, or even feign ignorance. Like all valley people, Sam Coyote could see right through them, the problem with those two, is that usually they could see through him as easily.

Sam Coyote had a pretty good idea of how the sheriff would handle it. He would say that it was a case of two young lovers eloping, despite there being no evidence that they knew each other. He would take this course of direction for two reasons. The first is that if he stuck to this story, the state officials would not get involved, and secondly it would buy him some time to tie it to somebody from the Plane.

Sam Coyote knew that at some point, he would have to deal with the spirits from the Plane who were doing this, but that could wait. There were reasonable people in the valley that he would be able to talk to. There was also that growing fringe outside of town that nobody of reason would be able to talk to. They wanted blood for the sake of blood. Nobody outside of their realm would ever be listened to.

Of all of the thoughts that were going through Sam Coyote's mind, the foremost was that he needed to speak to Margaret. He knew that she would be the most distraught over all of this. When he sat down nervously at the counter of the UFO Café, she tried hard to smile at him, but he saw that there was sadness in her eyes. She seemed to be spending an inordinate amount of time garnishing two plates that the cook had put up in the window.

After she delivered the plates to a young couple in the corner booth, she finally approached him, "Good morning, you know what you want to eat, or do you want to look at a menu?"

"I'm only going to have coffee today Margaret"

"Are you sure?"

"Yeah, I don't have much of an appetite today"

Margaret looked at him blankly. "Sam, I am a religious woman. I was born and raised an Irish-Catholic. There have been very few Sundays in my life that I haven't been to mass. I pray almost every minute of every day. I have always prayed for the people of the Plane as well as the people of the valley" She wanted to say more, but cut herself off.

Sam Coyote nodded affirmatively gently. "I know Margaret"

"I don't know what to pray for anymore"

"You can keep can praying for the same things you have always prayed for"

"Sam, those are just babies that are gone. We both know that they didn't run off together, that's the sheriff not wanting to get off his ass and look for them because they're Mexicans"

"I know that they didn't run off"

"Do you know what happened?"

"I talked to Ariel about it. We don't have any real answers, but I think we have an idea"

"We're they taken to the Plane?"

"I haven't heard for sure, but I don't see any other logical explanations"

"What's happening there?"

"The same thing that's happening in the valley, an influx of new souls that only have their own interests in mind. They're not interested in peace or harmony; they don't care about history. They have an overwhelming sense of entitlement. They want what they want, and they want it for themselves. There is no longer the thought that humanity is a collective whole, it's little groups that are collectively splintering away from everything else. Separatism is the only goal"

"It makes me sad Sam. I don't have a whole lot of road in front of me. I guess everything comes full circle. When I was a little girl, everybody was segregated. It was by race, or religion, or whatever they could think of. I thought we had moved beyond that. I guess I was wrong"

LXI

Fear is Contagious

Lola walked into Sam's place. He was sitting in an old rocking chair staring out the window at nothing in particular. She wasn't sure if he had heard her come in, so she started tiptoeing over to him. She didn't see him move, so she thought that he might be asleep. She was about a foot and a half away from shaking his shoulders.

"Nice try," he said. "I knew you were coming before I even saw your truck"

"I kind of figured, I guess I was kind of surprised that you weren't waiting for me at the door"

He stood up and hugged her, "How's my little girl?"

"I'm okay"

"Just some friendly advice," he looked at her to make sure she was listening, "now might not be a good time to go around sneaking up on people trying to surprise them"

"I know. I went and saw Lee today. He seemed kind of off, not himself"

"Yeah, I stopped in for coffee at Margaret's today. I don't think that I've ever seen her that way. She looked worried. I can't imagine the rest of the valley isn't worried too"

"Think about it from their perspective. Two kids of their kind are gone. They've heard the description of the last person to see the girl alive. An impeccably dressed older man with grey hair. It can be laughed off as an old myth or superstition, but there are some people in the valley, the old families, that are afraid of him. They say he's been coming here for hundreds of years and it's the same old story. He's friendly to a young woman, she attempts to seduce him and the girl was never seen again. Those people are afraid, and fear is contagious"

"I know you're right. If and when they find any bodies, things will turn ugly quickly.

Lola walked over and held Sam's hand. "If that happens there are going to be a lot people wanting some type of revenge"

Sam was perplexed. "By who?"

Lola was equally surprised at his reaction. "Sam, I don't mean any disrespect, it's becoming obvious that you are completely oblivious to what is going on. Jack's militia is growing in size"

"You've lost me. I don't know what the fuck you're talking about"

"Can I ask you a question?"

"Sure"

"What's the deal with you and Dimitrios?"

"What do you mean? There's no deal with me and Dimitrios"

"See Sam, you're in some kind of denial. Think about it, he showed up at your door, covered in blood after probably killing a bunch of people in Las Vegas and you treat it like it's nothing out of the ordinary, there is some kind of connection between you two"

"Have you noticed how nobody is looking for him? He's been pulled over twice by the cops since he's been here. They let him go"

"The news says there is nationwide manhunt under way"

"I haven't seen any sign of it. It's been a while now. They don't have an idea where he went. To the people looking for him, he's a ghost"

"So, you don't think he's the guy?"

"No, I know he's the guy. I haven't told anybody this, but I know Dimitrios from a long time ago. We've been on intersecting Planes before, and been on the same Plane before. The one thing I've learned about him, is that you wait until he starts to show his hand. If you think, at any time, that you have him figured out, that means you're about to get burned badly"

LXII

A Clean Soul

From the balcony at the Drive-In Inn, Dimitrios looked down at the projection house. He knew that there was somebody in there playing these scenes for a reason. The scenes on the screen kept getting more and more interesting. He wished that he had some popcorn, and maybe some Milk Duds with an extra-large Pepsi.

Dimitrios looked at the crumpled body of Andre York at the feet of Reverend Black. Then he looked at each of the four men still sitting in the room. "The four of you need to look at each other. Try to figure out which two are going to live, and which two aren't ever going home again" They all kept their eyes downward, ignoring what he said.

Dimitrios told Clint Black to stand up and walk over to the bar. "Would like a drink reverend?"

"I don't drink"

"Are you sure about that preacher? Now, might be a good time for you to do a shot"

"I like to maintain a clear head and a clean soul"

Dimitrios started laughing. "A clean soul? Is that what you fucking said to me?"

"Yes, it is. My savior requests that of me"

"Is Jesus your savior?"

"Yes, he is"

"Does Jesus know what a mother fucking scumbag you are? Does he know how you rip the elderly and the poor off so that you can in live in mansions and ride around in private jets"

"I do the work of the lord and he rewards me"

"Is that what you tell yourself asshole? Is that how you maintain a clear conscience? I remember hearing your daddy speak when I was a kid. He seemed to be an pious man. It amazes me that he could spawn a pariah like you"

"Unlike you sir, I know that my salvation is guaranteed"

Dimitrios walked over and stood in front of Clint. "Are you praying right now preacher?"

"Yes, I am"

"What are you praying for?"

"I am praying for divine intervention. I'm praying that my lord and savior touches your soul, shows you the wickedness of what are doing, and you will see the light and spare my life"

"So, let me get this straight. You're praying for yourself?"

"No, you don't understand. I'm praying for you"

"You're praying for me? You don't even fucking know me? That's pretty presumptuous of you. How do you know you're praying for the right thing?"

"How is praying for you to stop the slaughter not the right thing"

"Reverend, you're so fucked in the head and delusional that you have no idea what the right thing is. The right thing to you is whatever it takes to fill your bank account. You pray for yourself, you fucking scumbag"

"I am a man of God; I pray for all of humanity"

Dimitrios smirked and shook his head. "Reverend Black, are you starting to get the feeling that you aren't going to be one of the two that walks out of this room?"

The reverend started sobbing intensely, "Please. Please allow me to continue to do the work of God"

"Reverend Black, calm down, you should be happy right now"

"How can I be happy right now?"

"You're about to meet your savior" When Dimitrios pulled the trigger, for some reason the reverends skull exploded forward, instead of back. He had to use his sleeve to wash the blood from his face.

LXIII

Eating Vegetables

Sheriff Jack had sent his deputy, Matt, home for the evening. He was in no hurry to leave. He went to the break room and grabbed a beer out of the refrigerator. Back in his office, he kicked his feet up on his desk and slowly sipped from the can. He thought about the work that he could be doing, but in the moment didn't see the point of doing it. It would still be there in the morning.

When he heard the sound of a motorcycle pulling into the parking lot, he stood at the window, beer still in his hand, to see who it was. He couldn't tell, the rider had a bandana pulled up over his nose. Donovan held up his hands signifying he meant no harm. Only after the bike was parked and shut off, did the rider reveal his face. Jack recognized him, but didn't know him all that well. He knew that he was from the Plane, so he undid the strap on his holster. He snapped it back up, when he realized that he didn't feel threatened.

The sheriff had heard the stories of back in the day when Donovan would come into town to drink and raise a little hell. Those days had long passed Donovan by, he mellowed with age, at least when he was out in public. The sheriff watched him walk up to the front door, he pulled on it, but it was locked after Matt left. The sheriff was curious, so he went and opened the door.

"Is there something I can help you with?"

"Not really. I thought we could talk a little bit"

Jack was a bit perplexed. "What is it that you would like to talk about?"

"My gardening. I thought you might like to try some of my vegetables"

"No thanks, I'm not much of a vegetable guy" The sheriff started to shut the door.

"I've heard talk that you would like my vegetables"

The sheriff eyed him suspiciously. "Okay, I'm game. What kind of vegetables do you have?"

Donovan reached into the inside pocket of his leather jacket and pulled out a sandwich size ziplocked baggie of little brown buttons. "The boomer kind of vegetables"

"You know, I could arrest you right now for possession of a controlled substance"

"I know you could, but I also know that you won't"

The sheriff looked at his watch, then studied the parking lot for any other activity. "Come on in" Jack walked Donovan back to his office, pulled the blinds, and turned on the little lamp in the corner.

Donovan threw the bag across the desk to Jack. "Take as much as you want, I'll do the rest"

The sheriff half- laughed. "There's probably half an ounce in here"

"That sounds about right. What's your point?"

Jack grabbed a handful and put it into a pile in front of him, then slid the baggie back to Donovan who emptied it into a pile in front of him.

The sheriff put about half of the pile into his mouth. He chewed hard, and then eventually swallowed. He grabbed the beer to wash down the taste.

"You have another one of those beers?"

"Yeah," Jack said. He left the office, went to the breakroom and returned with the entire twelve pack.

The two men sat in silence with their eyes closed, slowly sipping on the beer until the mushrooms started to kick in.

"Holy fuck," the sheriff yelled. "They're here"

Donovan laughed, "I'm not too far behind you"

"So, tell me," Jack said. "Why did you come here with these?"

"I figured that this is the only way we could figure out what the hell is happening in this world. A psychedelic conference, if you will"

"That's pretty simple, and you don't need to trip to figure out that the Plane's people want to take over the valley and kill all the valley people"

Donovan started laughing, and then abruptly stopped. He stared at the sheriff intently for second. Then started laughing again, even harder, until there were tears rolling down his cheeks. "That's the stupidest thing I've ever heard of"

Jack was laughing too, his face leaving colored trails for Donovan. "I know it is, but it's the truth"

"No, it isn't. So, there's a few dead people. No big deal. It doesn't mean we want all of you dead"

"I'm going to let you in on a little secret. I don't care. There's a lot of people in this valley, and on the Plane as well, that need dying. I don't even know why I ran for this office. I don't care. I'm half tempted to build a little cabin in the mountains and live off the land"

Donovan raised his beer can. "I'll drink to that"

LXIV

On the House

Pride overwhelmed Dimitrios as he watched the Reverend Cliff Black's body crumble to the ground.

There were three people left alive in the suite. "Well, well, well, it looks like there is only one of you guy's left to die. Mr. James, would you like to nominate one of the idiots and tell me why you think they should die?"

Byron looked at the other two, then back up to Dimitrios. "You can just shoot me. I've lived a good life. Let these two gentlemen go"

Dimitrios looked at him quizzically, and smiled. "That's very honorable of you Mr. James. Let's see what these two have to say. Wayne Bloodsworth. Why don't you tell me who deserves to die"?

"You heard what Byron said. I nominate him, because he says he doesn't mind dying"

"You're a real fucking prick Wayne, you know that?"

"He said he wanted to die. You heard him. Let us go"

Dimitrios turned to Robert Christensen. "Bob, you have all of the power, so who's it going to be?"

"I honestly don't care. None of us deserve to die. None of these people lying on the floor deserved to die. Even you don't deserve to die. That said, since you are hellbent on killing some more, you decide who has to go don't put it on us"

"You honestly, truly don't care who lives or dies?"

"No. I've already watched these other people die. Do you think that one more head exploding is going to change anything? If you choose to shoot me, I won't have to see anymore killing"

Dimitrios walked over and poured some bourbon, then went back and handed it to Robert Christensen. "It's on the house"

"Thank you" He drink the entire glass in one movement.

"You're an enigma to me Mr. Christensen. I asked you the most important question you will probably ever be asked, I'm giving you the power over life and death, and you tell me that you don't care. Is that right? Am I understanding you correctly?"

"Yes, that sums it up"

"I read your shit, your racist, sexist bullshit. I see your videos about loving Nazis and hating Jews. I hear your rants about same-sex marriage. I've heard some fucked up shit come out of your mouth. You seem to care about that crap. You care about shit that will not affect your life in least, but when I ask you about life itself, you don't fucking care?"

"After what I've seen tonight, I don't think I have the ability to care anymore"

"Oh, how fucking convenient, an hour ago you were going to change the world, but now you don't care"

"That's right, I don't. Just shoot me"

"Okay"

After the shot rang out, Robert Christiansen's body slumped over on to Wayne Bloodworth's shoulder.

LXV

The Intersection

Sam woke up. He looked around. He was in his bed, but he wasn't in his room. He felt like he was floating somewhere. As he assessed his surroundings, it occurred to him that maybe he wasn't awake after all. He tried to swing his legs over to get out of bed, but he couldn't move. He tried to lift his arms, but they were paralyzed as well. He could blink his eyelids, but that seemed to be the extent of his movement.

Wherever Sam was, it was silent. Other than some source of light, that went from a blood red hue to a faint shade of pink, there was stillness to the place. He closed his eyes, trying go back to sleep but his paralysis was causing a surge of adrenaline that he could feel pumping through his veins. He wondered if he should be feeling some type of fear, but there was nothing there. There was a strange calmness.

Slowly rising, there was a sound, it sounded like wind blowing in the distance. It was coming from behind him. As the sound grew closer, he could feel a warm breeze blowing over him. There was another type of movement there too, it was footsteps. "Who's there?" he tried to say, but he had no voice.

His eyes rolled to the side of the bed; Ariel was standing there. She had no facial expression as she stared at Sam. She was naked, her long curly hair covered her breasts. She pulled the sheet off of his body. She sat down on the bed and started lightly dragging her fingernails over his chest. There was a tingling in his toes, then he felt it in the tips of his fingers. Slowly the tingling spread through the rest of his body, and it all came together where Ariel was touching him. When she leaned over to kiss him, the paralysis subsided and he was able to put his arms around her.

No words were spoken while the two of them made love for what seemed like an eternity. Although Sam and Ariel had known each other forever, in that moment, naked together on the bed, the two of them might has well have been strangers. They knew, as they interlocked with each other, that this was the beginning of a different kind of partnership than they had had in the past. As they lay there catching their breath, they both wondered what had happened.

"I believe this is some type of intersection' Ariel said.

"Why do say that?"

"Look around you Sam, we're in some kind of void. A blank canvas"

Between the earlier paralysis and making loving afterward, he never got a good look at where he was. There were no walls, just the reddish pink light that seemed to eventually fade into darkness. He looked in the direction of where he sensed Ariel coming from earlier.

"How did you get in here?"

"I don't know. I was meditating and got caught up in a dream"

"Do you still feel like this is a dream?"

"No, but I'm not sure we're in a tangible place either. Like I said earlier, it feels like an intersection"

"An intersection of different Planes?"

"Maybe, but usually when that happens, I feel it intently. This feels more subtle, like an intersection that's not supposed to be here" She took a deep breath and closed her eyes to the stillness. "It's an intersection filled with Zen, like everything that was supposed to happen all came together, but it is bisecting with some other force, an existential force. Something that is trying to take away all of the meaning"

He started kissing her. "We don't need to define it"

Ariel pulled Sam into her and the feelings of being familiar strangers that they had both felt earlier evaporated. As he propelled himself inside of her, he felt like he was connected to every cell in her body. She had her hands on his ass cheeks to pull him in tighter. They climaxed simultaneously and collapsed onto their backs.

Sam was out of breath. "I think I just got you pregnant," he said. Ariel didn't respond.

In the blink of an eye, he was back in his room. What the fuck? He got up and looked around the house. Everything was where it was supposed to be. He smiled, and said "What a crazy fucking dream that was" Throughout the day, he kept thinking about it. In the early afternoon Sam walked over to the spiritual center.

"Upstairs," Ariel called out from upstairs. When Sam got up there, she was watching a bumble bee on the floor. On the table were two cups of tea.

"Sit down" she said. "I've been expecting you"

"Listen, Ariel, I have to ask, did you have a strange dream last night?"

"We talked about that. We met at an intersection"

Sam wasn't surprised at her answer. "So that was real?"

"Yes, and by the way, you were right, and you did"

LXVI

Do you Believe in Irony?

Wayne Bloodsworth pushed Reverend Clint Black's body off of him, and let it fall to the couch. He stood up and stared at Dimitrios. "Thank you for sparing our lives," he said and started walking toward the door.

Dimitrios cocked the gun and aimed it him. "Wayne, sit the fuck back down"

"But you..."

"Wayne, I said to sit the fuck back down"

"You said you would let two of us live"

"What can I say Wayne. When I said that, I meant for you to be one of the first ones to go, but then it occurred to me that it was you, above all people, needed to see this whole thing unfold"

"What? Why me?"

Dimitrios held the gun up with his fingertips, and rotated it so that Wayne Bloodsworth could get a good luck. "Don't you recognize this gun?"

Wayne swallowed hard. "Where did you get that? Did the police give it to you?"

Dimitrios laughed, "You know, for the head of such an important group, you really are an idiot"

"Please, let me go. You promised. I have a wife and kids. I want to live"

"Oh, okay Wayne. You think I should let you live because you have a wife and kids? Is that what I understood?'

"Yes"

Dimitrios shook his head in disgust. "You know what Wayne, everyday more than a hundred people die from a gunshot wound in this country. Countless more are wounded. You don't think some of those people have wives and kids and families? Yet, somehow you made it your mission in life to get as many guns on the street as possible. I've heard you say that the problem in this country is that there aren't enough guns"

"I advocate for innocent people to be able to defend themselves against tyranny and injustice"

Dimitrios angrily went over and shoved the barrel of the gun into Wayne Bloodsworth nose with such force that it ripped the corner of his nostril. "You motherfucker! You can lie to your followers all you want. You can create an atmosphere of fear and scare them to death into sending you money so that you can pay off politicians and go buy those expensive suits that like to walk around in. But guess what fuck face. I have kids. They're still in elementary school, but there are days when they don't want to go to school. You know why that is Wayne? Because they're afraid of getting shot. They have to wear bullet-proof backpacks for fuck's sake"

"Sir, our group has a program designed to teach children gun safety and marksmanship. You can teach them to defend themselves"

Dimitrios rubbed his eyes in exasperation. "You do believe your own bullshit, don't you?"

"I believe in the truth"

"How about irony? Do you believe in irony Mr. Bloodsworth?"

"I guess"

"You should. Because in the not too distant future, people will look up the word irony and see your picture. The head of the biggest gun rights group got his head blown off by his own gun"

The bullet went straight up Wayne Bloodsworth sinus cavity and into his brain and out the back of his skull.

LXVII

An Old Cowboy

After Dimitrios watched the life bleed out of Wayne Bloodsworth, he looked over at Byron James. "Well sir, I guess I'm a man of half of my word. You can go"

Byron didn't move, he looked over the bodies strewn about the room. "I don't know if I deserve to live"

"Why is that?"

"As much as I like to think that I was different from all of the people at the convention, I wasn't"

"Why did you think you were different?"

"It was never my intention to be some type of hero. I wanted to be able to raise my cattle. That's all I ever wanted, it's in my blood to be a cowboy. I look back on the whole standoff with the federal agents, and still ask myself how things ever got that far. It was all a blur"

"To be honest with you Byron, I somewhat followed the whole standoff thing, and frankly I thought it was ridiculous. Any way I looked at it, it came down to cattle grazing on grass"

"That's all it was, until the government told me that I owed them a million dollars for letting cows onto their land. I tried to work with government; I wanted to know where they came up with that number. Next thing I know, there are snipers set up around my ranch"

"I thought I heard that you were in the one who set up snipers on your property"

"I didn't know those people. A bunch of anti-government militia types and agitators showed up. They told me that they were going to fight for my rights, and the rights of all people in the country. I guess that I got caught up in all of their bullshit"

"If that's true, then why are you here?"

"I don't know"

Dimitrios motioned Byron James up to the bar. "I could use a drink, how about you?"

"If you got Irish whisky, I could use a belt"

The two men toasted each other, and slammed back their shots. Dimitrios pulled the clip from the gun, inspected it, and slid the clip back in. "Tell me something Mr. James, are you here for the money or did you come to this convention for a bigger cause?"

"I'd like to say that it was for bigger cause, but I've already deposited the check, so I guess that tells you all you need to know. I don't have bigger causes; I'm just an old cowboy"

Dimitrios put the gun on the bar. "There are still two hollow points in the clip, and probably one in the chamber. The gun is yours to do as you see fit" He took another shot of whisky and walked towards the door. Without looking back, he said, "Byron, if you need to use that gun to stop me, I won't hold it against you"

There was no hesitation in Byron James voice. "Go"

Dimitrios walked down the hall from the suite. As he opened the door to the stairwell, he heard one last shot ring out.

LXVIII

Amen to That

The sound of an engine coming up the road to Sam's house had him thinking that it had to be the law. When he stepped outside, the last thing he expected to see was Margaret behind the wheel of her old Studebaker. She told Sam to get in. He was never one to tell her "no" for any reason.

He waited for her to say something, but he didn't want to interrupt her when it was apparent that she was driving with a mission. Once she got through Crestone, she stepped on the gas. When she finally had to stop to get onto the highway, he asked "What's going on Margaret?"

She looked at him and lowered her head. "Sam, I need to get out of the valley"

"Forever?"

"Oh Lord, no Sam Coyote, not forever. I could never leave my home for any length of time, but every now and then, when I'm fed up with something. I need to get up to a place high above the valley to clear my head"

"Where is that, Margaret"

"It's my special little place. It's about a couple hours up Highway 285, the other side of Kenosha Pass"

"What's there?"

"You'll see"

The two of them made comfortable small talk until they turned at Buena Vista, when Margaret put her hand on Sam Coyote's leg. "I want to tell you something" she said.

"Go ahead"

"I feel awful for the way I treated when you came into the café the other day. I know that in your heart you care about all of the people of the valley and the Plane. I went in the back and cried my eyes out after you left"

"Margaret, you know I love you, and you don't ever have to explain yourself. Tensions are ragged on both sides right now. The lunatic fringe from the valley is apparently running things there, there's some newcomers to the Plane that seem to thrive on chaos alone"

Margaret nodded and kept on driving, they reverted to mindless small talk again. They both wanted to say something that the other needed to hear, but neither one was willing to go first. It wasn't out of stubbornness; it was out admiration.

Margaret slowed down and turned across the highway and went down a short, but steep dirt road. The parking lot had a few other cars, and there were people taking pictures of the mountain side. Sam Coyote looked up, about halfway up the mountain was huge statue of Jesus, it must have been 50 feet tall. Below it, spelled out in big rocks painted white "Santa Maria"

Margaret grabbed his hand they started walking up the zig zag trail. It was a rough hike for a woman of her age, but she battled through it, stopping a couple of times for rest. She asked him if he had ever been there before. He told her no, and even though he had driven the highway a hundred times, he couldn't remember even noticing the place before.

The base of the statue was made of stones, and when she got there Margaret put the palm of her hand against one of them and prayed for several minutes. Sam walked around statue amazed at the quality of the sculpture.

Margaret came up behind him, "Thank you so much Sam Coyote for putting up with a dingy old lady like me, and coming with me here"

"It was my pleasure"

On the way back, once Margaret passed through Saguache she said, "Well, were officially back in the San Luis Valley"

"Yeah, it's strange. You can feel a different kind of atmosphere"

"Ever since I was little girl, I've told people that the world feels heavier here. It's as if there is some kind of harder pressure coming from the sky"

"One thing I know about the valley, Margaret, is that it has been here longer than anybody will ever realize, even before Earth was a planet, and it will be here long after the current inhabitants of the planet completely destroy it"

"Amen to that Sam Coyote, Amen to that"

LXIX

Two Black Eyes

Lola had made a routine out of watching for suspicious cars around the school. The old lady across the street was more than happy to let Lola watch from the living room, even making pie and tea on the days she felt up to it. Most afternoons were uneventful, the lady would teach Lola knitting on those days. Other times Lola interest was piqued by certain vehicle, and follow them only to discover there was an innocent reason for her curiosity.

Lola became a hawk over the school. A couple of times, she reported some fights to the school resource officer. One time she called an ambulance because one of the kid's mothers had OD'd on heroin right in front of the school. That day she had noticed a girl standing alone. She was the only one out there, all of the other kids had been picked up or rode the school bus home.

Lola walked across the street and asked if the girl was alright.

"I had to stay after school," the girl said. "My mom or dad were supposed to come pick me up, but I guess they got tired of waiting"

"What's your name honey?"

"Abigail"

Where do you live Abigail?

"On county road 116"

"Would you like for me to give you a ride home"

The girl looked away, and didn't say anything.

Lola looked at the girl, she could see a bruise on the girl's upper arm. "You can't stand out here all night" Lola said. "We can call somebody, or I can give you a ride home"

"Who would we call?"

"I don't know, you would have to tell me"

The girl looked as if she were about to cry. "Will you give me a ride home?"

"Of course"

Lola drove east on Highway 160, then turned south onto county road 116. There were no houses that Lola could see, only flat land covered by sage brush. "Are you sure this is the right road to your house Abigail?"

The girl looked around. "Yes"

"I don't see any houses out here"

"It's down a hill that you can't see from here. My dad said he wanted it that way"

Lola was immediately concerned at what the girl said. "Where does your dad work?"

"He's a sheriff's deputy"

"Oh, that's interesting. What's your dad's name?"

"Matt"

"Oh, I think I might know him" Lola tried to hide her disdain for the man.

The girl didn't say anything, but her hands shook the further they drove down the road.

"I was noticing the bruise on your arm. Did you get that at school?"

"No ma'am"

"What happened?"

"I was playing with the dog, and pulled me really hard" Lola knew that it was a lie that had been coached to her. The tone of voice lacked any kind of emotion.

The girl directed Lola where to turn, and eventually they pulled into a driveway that was somewhat hidden by trees. There, in a gulley, sat an old double wide trailer that from the outside looked as though it should be condemned. Two large dogs were on thick chains on either side of the door, one appeared to be Pit Bull-Mastiff mix, and the other was a scarred-up Rottweiler.

As Lola and the girl walked up to the door, a woman with a frantic look on her face opened it. She screamed at the dogs to stop barking. The woman was probably thirty, darkly complected, she had two black eyes, an off-center nose that was probably broken, and a lower lip that was split at least a good quarter inch.

"Your daughter somehow got left at school…."

The woman was pulled back from the door, and Matt appeared from behind. He was obviously drunk, tweaking on meth, and pointed a hand gun at Lola. He screamed for the Abigail to get in the house. Once she entered, he closed the door behind him and walked over and put the gun directly in Lola's face. "What the fuck are you doing on my property?"

She didn't flinch, she was challenging in her demeanor. "Obviously, you were too drunk and methed up to pick up your own daughter from school, so somebody had to get her home. If, that's what you want to call this place"

"I should arrest you for trespassing right now"

"Why don't you go ahead and call your sheriff. Let him see how badly you beat your family"

Matt pulled the hammer back on the gun. Lola took a step closer to him. "You know that if you even think about pulling that trigger, you will disappear from this place, because you aren't the only law around here" Five bikers pulled on the berm above the driveway.

The deputy thought about it, and lowered the weapon.

As Lola walked away, she turned around one last time.

"You might disappear anyway"

LXX

The Manassa Mauler

Sam looked at Lola as they drove down Highway 285. He could tell that something was bothering her. He thought about asking her, but didn't. If she wanted him to know, she would say something. The silence continued as they passed through La Jara. When Sam got to the town of Romeo, he turned east.

Sam drove down the next town's Main Street until he came to a little red cabin with the statue of boxer in front of it. He stopped the car and got out. Lola followed him.

"The Manassa Mauler!" Sam said to himself.

"Who was he?" Lola asked.

"Jack Dempsey. He was the heavyweight boxing champion from 1919 to 1926. He was vicious, a one-man wrecking machine. The first boxer to ever have a million-dollar fight. There are a lot of people who would argue that he is the greatest boxer in history."

Lola looked up at the bronze statue of a muscular man striking a boxing pose. It stood atop a granite base. She read the inscription. "Why is the statue dedicated to his mother?" she asked.

"From everything I've heard, she was the stability of his life. The family was extremely poor. His father had a tough time finding work and the family moved a lot, and Jack didn't much care for his dad. Because they were so poor, he eventually became a boxer. When the family was having trouble putting food on the table, The Manassa Mauler would go into saloons and tell the men in there that he couldn't sing or dance but he could beat the shit out of any son of a bitch in the bar. Eventually some drunk would take him up on the challenge and Dempsey would kick his ass. The story goes that he never lost any of those fights."

Lola looked at Sam, then back to the statue. "There's a reason that you brought me here," she said. "There's a reason for everything that you do."

"Why were you so quiet on the drive down here?"

"I was at the deputy's house yesterday. He's such a fucking asshole. I can't stop thinking about his family. His wife and kids seem so miserable. I feel bad for them."

"I guess that is part of the reason for bringing you here."

"What do you mean?"

"There is something about Jack Dempsey that has always fascinated and inspired me, not because he was from around here. I like the way that he conducted himself. He was a nasty brawler and tough as nails, but he was also a gentleman. He didn't just fight for the sake of fighting the way some men do."

"What does that have to do with the deputy and his family?"

"Dempsey was righteous fighter. He did it for the right reasons. I see a lot of that quality in you."

"I like to think that I am that way too, but after yesterday I feel weak. Those people shouldn't have to live that way. I feel like I have failed them. They need help"

"Lola," Sam put his arm around her and they leaned on the base of the statue. "The last thing that you are is weak. To the contrary, you are one of the strongest people that I know. I wasn't sure what to expect after Victor got killed"

"I know, I want everything to be perfect and I want everybody to be happy."

"That is noble of you. It's not very realistic, but it is noble and that is what I love about you."

"I have to do something to help them."

"Again, that is noble. I'm not sure that you are seeing the bigger picture."

"What is the bigger picture?"

"Deputy Matt isn't shit. He's a peon. He's a symptom. He is by no mean the cause."

Lola nodded her head in agreement but didn't say anything.

"The reason I came here," Sam continued, "is because I needed a little inspiration, and I thought you could use some too. I'm getting the feeling that there is a big fight ahead of us."

"I have been feeling that way too, I'm not sure what it is that I'm supposed to be fighting."

"I'm not sure what is either, but it needs to create a paradigm shift"

"You're right. I guess that I don't want to believe it right now."

LXXI

The Filter on the Portal

Lola walked into the UFO café to find it deserted except for Margaret and Lee. They were sitting at the counter with coffee mugs in front of them. They both looked up and smiled when they saw Lola.

"Why, Lola, what a pleasant surprise," Margaret said as she walked over and gave her a hug. Lee got up and gave Lola a kiss on the cheek.

"How are you two doing this fine day?" Lola asked.

"A cup of coffee with an old friend," Lee said, "what could be better than that?"

"Oh my," Margaret said. "Lee, you know that flattery goes straight to my head."

Lola laughed.

"What brings a beautiful young lady into see up couple of old buggers like us?" Lee asked.

"Speak for yourself Lee." Margaret said.

"Sam and I went down to Manassa yesterday," Lola said. "We went to the Jack Dempsey statue and started talking about fighting. One thing led to another and we started talking about some of the things that are going on around here. Both of us are a little concerned about what we are seeing."

"Well, Lola," Lee said. "You aren't the only one is a little bit on guard about what is happening around here. A lot of the old timers won't speak about it openly, but believe me, there are many whispers being heard around this valley."

"Lee is right," Margaret said. "I would go even a little further by saying its more than a few whispers. I think it's bigger than that. There are many people around here that are downright afraid. They are leaving there house only when they need to. I've had to throw out a lot of the café's food before it spoiled. It's a good thing that this old place is paid for. I don't think that I would be able to stay in business if people don't start coming out"

"What are they the people whispering about?" Lola asked.

Lee and Margaret looked at each other. "They're worried about the Plane," Lee said. "For the most part, it has always been a comfortable relationship between the two worlds. Many of the folks around here don't think that is the case anymore."

"Let's be fair Lee," Margaret interrupted. "There are a few bad elements from the valley as well. Lola, honey, I don't think that filter to the portal is working the way that it is supposed to. You've got the militia riding around like the gestapo, and the bikers waiting to make their move"

"I don't understand," Lola said. "What do you mean the 'filter to the portal?"

"You don't know about the portal?" Lee asked.

"No."

"Lee," Margaret said, "She needs to know about the portal."

"I guess you're right, but I don't want to step on Sam Coyote's toes"

"Don't worry about Sam," Lola said.

The three of them went out to Lee's old Chevy Blazer and started driving a little road up the San Juan's. There was an unease in the car. After about a half hour of driving in the mountains above the town, Margret stopped the car.

"I've never been up here before," Lola said. "Is this it?"

"Most of the people who know about this place think it's an old mineshaft." Lee said.

"That's what it looks like to me." Lola said.

"It's so much more than that Lola," Margaret said. "It's a portal into all space and time. You can access any Plane or dimension by going into that shaft."

"How do you know that?" Lola asked.

"Legend has it," Lee explained, "that the people of the valley have known about it for hundreds, if not thousands, of years. The story goes that there was a tribe of Indians here several hundred years ago, and another tribe made it through this portal. A great vicious battle ensued, and many lives were lost. I talked to a Ute medicine man that said the Pueblo Indians came here after leaving Mesa Verde. After that, a great holy man of the tribe here was able to put an incantation on the portal to keep evil from entering the valley again."

"Those that have made it through over the years have been peaceful," Margaret said. "There has been serenity here because of the incantation. Lately though, the people that are whispering in the valley have wondered of the spell that old Indian put on it has worn off."

"The spell hasn't always been perfect Margaret and you know it," Lee said. "There have always been a few bad apples that have made it through."

"I suppose," she conceded. "We weren't even sure about Sam Coyote at first"

"Is there anything that can be done about it?" Lola asked.

"Nobody knows," Lee said.

"It takes a brave soul to go down there," Margaret said. "As far as anybody knows, nobody that has ever went down there has come back."

Lola walked over to the shaft and looked down. She could see a ladder descending into the darkness. She looked back at Lee and Margaret. "Thank you so much for showing me this. It gives me a lot to think about"

LXXII

What Needs to be Done

Lola walked into Sam's house. She was taken away by the feeling of the place. There was an eerie stillness in the air. She stopped in her tracks and listened for a few moments. There was not a sound to be heard. She walked back to the door and looked out. His truck was still out front.

"Sam?" she called out. There was no answer. She walked down to see if the door to the tunnels to see if it looked like it had been used, it didn't look like it.

"Sam, are you here?" She called out again, this time a little bit louder. Still, there was no response. She walked up the stairs, to see if he was there. There in the chair was Sam sitting in the big chair that faced the bay window looking out over the valley. She approached carefully as she was not sure what she was going to find. Sam was sitting there with his eyes wide open looking out to the west.

"Sam, are you okay?"

Sam looked up at her. He had a strange look in his eye, like he was in some kind of trance. He didn't say anything.

"Sam. What is the matter?"

He finally looked up at her, but for a brief moment he didn't appear to recognize her. Then in an instant he smiled, and breathed out sigh of relief. He smiled. "Lola, my angel." He stood up and gave her a hug.

"Are you okay, Sam?"

"Yeah. I got lost a little too deep in thought."

"What were you thinking about?"

He put his arm around her and guided her over to the window and stared out over the brush of the valley. "I think we both know the answer to that."

"Yeah, I guess we do."

"So, what brings you here today my love?"

"Do you know about the portal in the mine shaft outside of town?

Sam rolled his eyes and he studied Lola for a while. "Yeah. How do you know about?

"How come you never told me about it?"

"I was going to. Someday. I never thought it was the right time, but you never answered my question: How do you know about it?"

"Lee and Margaret took me up there."

"Why?"

"I went to into the café yesterday. I told them about our trip to the Jack Dempsey statue. We started talking about some of the forces in the valley, and they decided that it was time for me to see it."

"I guess I should have taken you up there sooner. I was worried about how you would use it"

"Have you ever been through it?"

"Yes."

"And?"

"And what?"

"What did you think of it?"

"It's easy to get lost in there?"

"Lee and Margaret said nobody has ever come back from there."

"That's not true. I'm standing here in front of you."

"Tell me about it."

"There aren't words. It's indescribable."

"The two of them said there used to be a filter on it to protect the valley."

Sam thought about it for a while before saying anything. "I would say that the forces today are a lot different than they used to be."

"In what way?"

"I don't know. They just are. People used to care about one another, no matter what"

"I get the feeling that Lee and Margaret think that the portal is the key to stopping the battle for the valley. Do you think that's true?"

"I think that there is going to be a battle anyway. Some of the bad forces are already here, and they aren't going back."

"You think it's too late, Sam?"

"I didn't say that. Maybe the portal is the long-term answer, but there is an immediate war that needs to be fought first."

"You are not going to like this, but I need to see what the portal is about."

"Lola…"

"Sam, please. We both know that this needs to be done."

The two of them drove in silence as they made their way up to the old mine shaft. The sun was setting when they got there. Sam parked the truck and the two of them walked over and looked down the shaft. Deep down inside they could see that there was a faint light far down below.

"You don't have to do this, Lola."

"Yes. Yes, I do Sam. I love this valley and the people in it. I have to do something. Victor is expecting me"

"You are a good soul."

"I love you, Sam."

"I love you."

Sam and Lola didn't lose eye contact until she got too far down the ladder.

LXXIII

A Fog of Destiny

There was nothing about the images on the screen that surprised him. Ever since the day that he pulled into the valley, he knew that this day would eventually have to come. Dimitrios paused for a moment and realized that it had been a long time that he felt this type of calmness. There was a fog of destiny in the atmosphere.

Although the sun was well above the horizon, Dimitrios looked through the curtains in hopes that there would be some more images on the screen. He hoped for one last glimpse of the images that he left behind in his life in Las Vegas before he decided to gun all of those people down in the casino. He wanted to see a celluloid image of the face of his young bride. He thought about his children and wondered how they were doing.

He went to the closet and grabbed his gun. He ejected the clip to make sure it was full, then pushed it back into the gun. He walked to the bed and rested his head on the pillows that were stacked up against the head board. There was nothing left to do but wait. All Dimitrios could do was listen and wait.

It wasn't long before he could hear the sound of tires driving over gravel. There were several cars in the parking lot. Engines turned off. Truck doors slammed in rapid succession. There were footsteps, moving slowly. In the midst of it, he could make out the sound of the pump on a shotgun putting a shell into the chamber. The footsteps started coming up the stairs. He lifted his head from the pillow, and moved until he was sitting at the foot of the bed. Dimitrios cocked his gun.

Motorcycles could be heard for miles around.

He expected the knock that came at the front door. He was

not expecting the one that came from the big wooden door that led

to the tunnels. He ignored the front door, and opened the back.

Sam Coyote walked through the back door. He was holding a

machine gun in his hands, and had a sawed-off double barrel

strapped to his waist.

"What are you doing here?"

"There was a knock at your front door."

"I know that there was."

"It's Sheriff Jack, and his deputy Matt. They brought the

militia too"

"I know that too."

"Don't you think that you should open it?"

There was another knock at the front door. Sam nodded towards it. Dimitrios walked over and pulled the door open. Jack rushed it, knocking Dimitrios back. Matt ran in pointing the gun in Dimitrios' face. Sam fired a couple of shots from the machine gun into the ceiling of the motel room startling the sheriff and his deputy.

Jack looked at Sam. "This has nothing to do with you."

"I wouldn't be here if I didn't think it didn't have everything to do with me."

Jack nodded towards Dimitrios. "This man killed a lot of my friends in Las Vegas."

"If you were here to arrest me, it would seem that the parking lot would be filled the FBI and every other lawman for the surrounding two hundred miles." Dimitrios said, "not a bunch of rednecks with pitchforks"

All four men raised their weapons. "I'm not here in a law enforcement capacity," Jack said. "I'm here for revenge. Several of my brothers are dead."

Sam aimed the machine gun at Jack. "One of you might get a shot off, but one of you is going to die. You have been terrorizing in this valley for far too long."

Jack shifted his aim from Dimitrios to Sam. "I've been protecting this valley that long. There are three dead hikers, and a mutilated kid from Monte Vista. What was left of him was found in a hog pen. The girl is still missing. Mexicans have been overrunning this place. I've been protecting the valley from the Plane. You are all savages."

A shot rang out. It came from Dimitrios' gun. Blood exploded from Jack's neck as he collapsed to the ground. Several shots came rapidly from Sam's gun. Two bullets struck each of Matt's kneecaps. He dropped the shotgun and collapsed on the bed screaming in agony.

Gunfire rang out from the parking lot. Sam handed the machine gun to Dimitrios and walked over and stood over Matt. He pulled the sawed-off shotgun off of waist, pulled back both hammers and aimed it at Matt.

"Please," Matt screamed. "I don't deserve this"

Sam smiled. "If you hurt little kids, and torture your family, you deserve it." Both barrels of the shotgun went off.

Sam grabbed Dimitrios by the elbow and walked out into the tunnel. Sam yelled out, "We're going to need maid service in there."

They could hear the helicopters coming.

LXXIV

A Good Fire

Donovan sat in the big log chair next to the stone fire place. The reflection of the flames danced off of his face. "This is nice, Sam. I'm glad that you talked me into doing this."

"How are you feeling my old friend?"

"The pain is always there, sometimes I can barely take it." Dimitrios looked around the room. "The Platoro Lodge. This place brings back so many memories. I'll bet that if I made a list of the 25 best memories, probably half of them would involve this place, or at least in the forest around here. Getting lost while hiking down to that lake. Catching that monster rainbow out of the reservoir. Riding motorcycles on the trails around here. That was a whole different lifetime ago."

Sam smiled. "This is a great place. I love it here."

"I spent my honeymoon here," Donovan said. "I brought Julie here. She loved it as much as I did. She was so beautiful. We spent every day hiking these woods. At night, we made love until the guests in the other room banged on the walls and sent the front desk up to ask us to quiet down. Donovan went silent for a while. A tear streamed down his face. "I fucked that marriage up."

"I remember Julie," Sam said. "She was a nice girl. I always liked her."

"Do you remember the first time that we came here, Sam?"

Sam thought about it for a minute. "Geez, Donovan, we've been coming up here forever."

"Come on Sam, think."

Sam stood up and walked over to fireplace. He grabbed a log from the mantle, and through it on the flame. "Give me a hint."

Donovan laughed. "Chocolate chip pancakes."

Sam laughed along with his friend. "Oh yeah, it was the summer between fourth and fifth grade. Your stepdad brought us up here. What was his name again?"

"Winston."

"Oh yeah. I'll never forget him asking what I wanted for breakfast. I told him that I didn't care. He asked if I was sure, and I said yeah. The next thing I know we were eating chocolate chip pancakes. I pretended that I thought it was gross, but secretly thought they were delicious."

"I did too," Donovan smiled. "But there was no fucking way I was going to let Winston know that."

"Do you remember the fishing those few days?"

"Of course. We were catching a beautiful little brookies on every cast."

The two of them sat there in silence for close to a half hour before Donovan finally spoke again. "Like I said, my old friend Sam, that's like an entirely different lifetime. Sometimes, I wonder if it was even me that lived those times. Maybe I have hijacked somebody else's memory."

"How are you feeling Donovan?"

"You and this place make the pain almost bearable."

"Can I get you anything?"

"Sam, you know the end is near, right?"

"I know."

"I don't have the fight in me anymore."

"There's nothing wrong with that."

"After so much fear, I'm actually looking forward to see what's coming next."

"There are a lot of endings that have happened. Both on the Plane, and in the valley."

"Oh, yeah?"

"Jack and Matt are dead. We killed them. Their bodies were burned in the tunnel."

"Good. I never met bet a couple of bastards that had it coming more than those two, but I have a question."

"What?"

"Who's 'we"?

"It happened at the Drive-In Inn. In Dimitrios' room."

Donovan lowered his head and shook it. "Fuck, Sam, do you trust that guy?"

"No."

"Well, I guess what's done is done."

"That's not all, my friend."

"What else?"

"Lola left"

"Where did she go?"

"Into the portal."

"You let her go?"

"Come on, Donovan. We both know that there's a dark cloud above the valley and the Plane."

"I know. But still, you let Lola go into the portal?"

"You know how idealistic she is. How she wants everything to be perfect and how she wants everybody to be happy. She thinks she can bring cohesion back to the valley"

"Well, if anybody can bring back the peace to everybody, it's her."

"I know."

Sam walked over and sat by the fire. He held his hands to the flames to warm them. He picked up the poker and rearranged the logs. They cracked and popped, but it pushed a wave of heat into the room.

"There is nothing quite like a good fire, is there buddy?"

When Donovan didn't respond to him, Sam looked over at his friend. His head was tilted to his shoulder, and there was a slight smile on his face.

"Rest well my friend."

Sam walked out onto the porch. Orbs danced in the sky.

LXXV

Two Tuxedoes

The bar in the tunnel would normally be packed this time of day. Instead, it was only Sam and the bartender.

"You are looking rather dapper tonight, Mr. Coyote," the bartender said.

"Call me Sam, and thank you."

"I don't think that I have ever seen you in tuxedo before. What can I get you to drink?"

"Just get me a bourbon and water."

Sam could feel a figure approaching from behind. He looked over his shoulder and saw Dimitrios walking towards him. He also was dressed in a tuxedo. The bartender asked what he would be having before he sat down.

Dimitrios looked across the shelf of liquor. "Get me a double vodka and soda with a little bit of lime juice in it."

"Let's go sit at a table?" Dimitrios said.

Sam looked at him, then looked back down at his drink. "I guess."

"Wait for me to get my drink."

The two of them settled into the furthest, darkest table in the back.

"I didn't know if you would be going to the party tonight," Dimitrios said.

"Well, if there is one thing that Lilith is good at, it is throwing a party. Things tend to get pretty crazy when she is in charge."

"I do think that it's odd she insisted that everyone wear formal wear, but hey, if she is going to pay for it, I'm game."

"Dimitrios, if you wanted to talk about the party, we could have sat at the bar."

"I wanted you to know, I'm grateful for what you did the other day."

Sam stood up from his chair and looked down into Dimitrios' eyes. "I'm going to get us another round."

When he returned to the table and resumed staring into those eyes. "Tell me, Dimitrios, what is it that you think the other day was about?"

"Jack and Matt were going to kill me for what I did to their friends in Las Vegas."

"Why do you think they didn't just arrest you? They could have killed you later."

"I don't think upholding the law was something that ever interested either one of them."

"Why do you think that I showed up?"

"That, Sam, is something that I have been thinking about quite a bit the last couple of days. I have a few guesses, but I would rather hear it directly from your mouth. So, tell me, why did you come help me?"

"Dimitrios, you don't understand what's going on around here at all, do you? I didn't come to help you at all?

"Then why did you show up at my door?"

"I knew that it was perfect chance to kill the sheriff and his deputy. I've been waiting a long time for that chance."

"Why?"

"You're right. They don't give the first damn about the law. They came here as assassins a few years back and never left. When the Las Vegas assassins in Vegas didn't get you, they knew the shooter would be heading this way."

"So, does everybody know who I am?"

"Not everybody, there's just a couple of us. Most people aren't sure what to make of you. Everybody wonders what your motive is here. We all believe that there is a reason that you're here. You didn't show up here by accident."

"The truth is, Sam, I'm not sure why I'm here myself. Why doesn't the whole world know my name. It's like nobody is even looking for me. I'm not even sure how I got here. It's blur with a few vivid visions. The first is me taking one last look at bodies on the floor in the suite and running down the stairwell. Then I see myself driving across the desert and getting swallowed up by a sandstorm. Then I'm driving up to your house. I thought to myself, 'this is the place.' I still don't know why I thought that. I have this recurring dream that I am a giant bird"

"The Plane was already on edge before you got here."

"Why is that?"

"It wasn't long before you got here, that Lilith showed up. They feel same way about her that the feel you. She showed up out of nowhere, and took the place by storm. She has a strong soul."

"Yes, she does." Dimitrios looked down at his watch. "And that is exactly the reason we should start making our way over to the party."

"Dimitrios, sooner than later, you and Lilith will find out whether this Plane is the destination you are supposed to be in."

"I have a feeling that the subject will come up at the party tonight"

Sam looked at Dimitrios, then stood up and walked out.

LXXVI

The Surprise

Lilith greeted Sam Coyote and Dimitrios as they walked through the door. "Where have you been, the party's ready already in full swing."

"We stopped at the bar for drinks," Dimitrios said.

Sam looked around the room. He was surprised at some of the guests that he saw. Most of them were elderly. They were all dressed in formal dress, but most of the fashion was from decades ago. He was also taken aback that Lilith would throw a party where the music was provided by a lone cellist in the corner.

Lilith walked over to him and locked her elbow under his. "Don't worry Sam," she whispered. "I wanted everybody to be invited, but I'm not naïve enough to think that a good party is a one size fit all affair. The real party is downstairs around the hot spring. Let's go get you two a drink and I will take you down."

With drink in hand, the three of them made their way down the winding, stone staircase. The smell of Sulphur getting stronger by the step. The sound of horn-heavy jazz made its way up. When they reached the bottom landing, Lilith turned and faced Sam and Dimitrios then slid the straps of her dress and let it fall to the floor. She stood nude in front of them. The two men looked around the pools deck. Clothing was piled up on the floor. Everybody in the pool was naked. "I love getting dressed up in fine clothing," Lilith said. "I just don't like to be in it long."

She nodded at Sam and Dimitrios, who didn't catch her cue. She walked over and started untying Dimitrios bow tie. "I like to look at other people in fine clothing too. Just not for long."

Once the two men were naked, she led them to a part of the hot spring that had a private room built around it. Inside, floor to ceiling window looking over the valley twinkling in the dark below. The room had its own bar, and a stone framed bed next to fireplace off to the side. The room was illuminated only by candlelight and torches fixed to the wall.

"You two get in the water. I'll get us some more drinks and be back in a minute."

As soon as she walked into the water she waded over and straddled Dimitrios. She kissed him long and deep. "I've been waiting to do this all day, baby." She started grinding on him and moaning. The movements got more and more furious. Lilith's moans turned to screams. Sam smiled as he watched the two of them fuck.

After the two of them had cum, it took seemingly forever for them to catch their breaths. Lilith's head rested on Dimitrios shoulder. She stared at Sam as her breathing slowly subsided. "I have a surprise for you, Sam."

"I'm not sure if I should be excited or terrified."

Lilith lifted her head and stared even more intently. "That's a good question, Sam."

"I guess I'll take my chances."

"I think you are going to like this surprise. One thing I've learned about you is that you have a dirty mind. You don't let anybody onto that, you're always the perfect gentleman. But you have a nasty soul."

"I'm intrigued."

Lilith stood and made her way up to the deck. "I know what you like, and you are going to like this. I'll go find her." Lilith walked out of the private room, into the room where the party was going on.

Sam looked at Dimitrios. "Do you know what this is about?

He nodded. "Yeah, I do."

"What's this all about?"

"You know Lilith. She does want to give you a surprise. But true to her style, she's in it for her motive."

"This is true."

"She likes to entertain herself."

"I think you did a pretty good job of entertaining her too."

"I've never met any woman that likes to fuck as much as Lilith does."

"Yeah, I would agree with that."

It wasn't long before Lilith returned from the party. She was holding hands with a girl, who had the most devilish smile on her face. She was a Mexican girl, tall and lean with long legs. Her skin was suntanned dark, and without a blemish. Straight, shiny jet-black hair flowed down to her lower back.

Lilith had the girl stand at the top of the stairs and pose. "What do you think of your surprise, Sam? Her name is Valentina"

"She's beautiful."

LXXVII

Imposing Your Will

As she stood at the top of the stairs, Lilith came over and started rubbing the girl's body. She kissed the girl's neck, before moving to her lips. Lilith's kissing started going lower, the chin, the nape of the neck, before settling in on the nipples. The girl bit her lip, Lilith kissed her breasts.

Lilith moved behind the girl and kissed her back, her rubbed the girl's stomach. The girl started grinding ass into Lilith. As they found rhythm to their movement, Lilith's hand found her way to the girl's clit, showed rubbed it slowly at first, but she increased the pulse until the girl was shuddering in orgasm.

"Go lay down and rest on the bed," Lilith told Valentina.

Lilith walked into the pool and sat side ways on Sam's lap, "What do you think of your surprise, Sam?"

"I'll give you credit, you do know what I like."

Lilith stood up and pulled Sam up with her. She guided him up the stairs, "Let's go get you two acquainted." As she approached the bed, she noticed Sam's hard dick. She grabbed it, and guided him to the edge of the bed. She started stroking, then she went down, and kissed the head before eventually deepthroated him. She pulled the girl over, and put her head on Sam's dick. She gently pushed at the back of the girl's head.

Dimitrios was getting jealous.

"I think it's time for you to fuck her, Sam. Do you want to fuck her?

"Oh yeah, you know I do." He pulled the girl up, then positioned her on the bed. As he crawled on, Lilith pulled at his shoulder.

"That's not how you want it."

"What do you mean?"

"Get up," she said. "I'll show you how you want it." Lilith

pulled a strap from the corner of the bed. She put the cuff of the

strap on the girl's right wrist, cinching it to make sure that it was

tight. She walked to each corner of the bed and did the same to the

other limbs. "That's what you want, isn't it Sam? You want to be

able to be able to impose your will on her, don't you?"

Sam smiled.

"See," Lilith continued. "I know what goes on in that nasty

soul of yours. On the inside, you are a savage. Do anything you

want to her. Be as savage as you were to that hiker"

"You were pretty savage as well"

Sam crawled on to the bed, and kneeled between the girls

subdued legs. Her put three fingers into the girl, and thrust them

hard. Valentina had little reaction. Sam inserted his dick into her

and violently slammed himself into her. He looked over at Lilith,

"Take of the cuffs."

When the girl was free, Sam rolled her over onto her stomach. He spit on his finger, and used it to lubricate the rim of the girl's ass. He then put more spit on his finger and spread over his dick and put it into the girl. When he was done sprayed his cum on the girl's ass. He laughed and got off of the bed.

Lilith walked over to Sam and stared at Sam without saying anything.

"That was fun, Lilith. Thanks for the surprise."

"I'm sure it was."

He could feel her darting stare. "Is something wrong?"

"That's the last time you impose your will on anybody on this Plane."

"What do you mean?"

"Your time in this destination has come to an end."

"This my Plane."

"Not anymore."

"And how do you plan to get me to leave?"

Lilith nodded to Dimitrios. He walked over to bed and grabbed the girl by her hair, and pulled her head back. From under a towel, Dimitrios pulled out a large silver knife and drug the blade across the girl throat. He lay her down and plunged the knife into the girl's heart.

"Do you know who she was, Sam?"

He was shaking at what he had witnessed. "No, I don't."

"It's the girl that's missing out of the valley. We've been using her as fuck toy, but I knew she would eventually have a higher purpose. What will the people of the valley think if they knew you did this to the poor girl?"

Sam looked at Lilith, then over to Dimitrios, and back to Lilith. "Why?"

"It's what I've been saying all night. You are not who you say you are. You're a dark soul, that you have been able to hide for so many years, but people are seeing through you. This party tonight was for the people of the Plane to celebrate your departure."

Sam nodded his head in agreement. He walked out into the night, naked.

LXXVIII

Into the Light

Sam kept an old wooden ladder by the side of the house.
There was no sense in putting it too far away given the frequency at
which he would have to climb up on the roof to fix a leak. A house
that old was bound to have them. He propped the ladder against
the house and climbed up. He scaled his way to the highest point of
the roof. He sat there and looked around the valley. He looked
behind him at the towering peaks of the Sangre De Christo
Mountains. He thought about all of the times that he waited for
sun to come over those peaks to warm the valley.

Far across the valley was the majestic San Juan Range of the Rockies. As the sun would set over them it would create a spectrum of colors on the snow-covered mountains. From the top of his roof, he tried to name all of the little towns that sparsely populated the valley. The bigger ones, like Alamosa and Monte Vista were easy. Some of the tinier ones he had trouble remembering their names. A tinge of melancholy came over him. This had been his home for so long, after the initial shock, he knew that it was time for him to go.

He climbed down the ladder. As soon as his feet hit the ground, he heard a voice. "Are you taking one last look?"

Sam Coyote turned around to see Ariel standing there. "Yes," he said. "I guess that was the last time."

"Where are you going?"

"How did you know that I was leaving?"

"Lilith had a party."

"I know. I was there. I don't recall seeing you there."

"I wasn't. I received an invitation, but I didn't think I should go. I know why Lilith has parties. They mean that somebody is going away."

"Yeah, it's probably a good thing that you weren't there. I knew that she would make me the guest of honor one of these days."

"I'm sure that she will be having another party in the not too distant future, and when the invitation is sent to me, it will come with some insistence that my presence will be required."

"I'm assuming that once I am gone, she will view you as her main threat. Are you going to meet her challenge? You're the only one left that can beat her."

"I'm not going to give her the pleasure. I've become too complacent on this Plane. I've done all that I can do here. I'm going to find a place where my soul can continue to grow."

"Where are you going to go?

She thought about it a moment before answering. "I'll know the right destination when I find it, so it's not a matter of where, but what method do I use to get there."

"Lola went down the portal not too long ago. She wanted to find a way to help the people of the Plane and the valley."

Ariel sighed, "she may be their only hope."

"I think I'm going to follow her. It will be a nice walk from here."

She walked over to the ladder and climbed up it. She went just high enough to see the entire valley, even those to the south. She stood for a few minutes, then climbed back down."

"I'm ready for that walk now," she said.

When they got to the portal, it was not like when Lola went down and there was a faint light deep down in the pit. The old mine shaft looked like there was a searchlight in its belly. It made a beam into the skies. It was visible even in the sunlight.

There was no hesitation as Sam and Ariel descended into the light. About halfway down the ladder they stepped off to fall directly into the light. Eventually they passed through the light end drifted down a stream of total darkness. They floated at a gentle pace for what seemed like an eternity.

Slowly, the subtle hint of light began to seep up the tunnel. As the light grew, the stream started to transform and Sam Coyote and Ariel found themselves walking on a cobblestone path running the middle of a wild flower patch. They were in the middle of an island. The sea was a half mile down from them in any direction.

They faced each other. As they looked in to each other's eye, he asked, "is that you?" She put her index finger straight up over her lips. He watched she walked over to a bumble bee that was struggling on the stone. She held a blade of grass to the bee. With a little prodding from her, the bee grasped on to the green blade. She lifted it up, and rested it in the center of the flower.

Sam Coyote went over and rubbed Ariel's belly.

www.ingramcontent.com/pod-product-compliance
Lightning Source LLC
Chambersburg PA
CBHW060339260626
47160CB00006B/2136